Valery the Great

Elaine McCluskey

VALERY
the GREAT

★ STORIES ★

Anvil Press Publishers Inc.
P.O. Box 3008, Main Post Office
Vancouver, B.C. V6B 3X5 Canada
www.anvilpress.com

Library and Archives Canada Cataloguing in Publication

McCluskey, Elaine, 1955–
     Valery the great / Elaine McCluskey.

Short stories.
ISBN 978-1-897535-89-9

     I. Title.

PS8625.C59V34 2012   C813'.6   C2012-901156-8

Cover design: Rayola Graphic Design
Front cover illustration: Carl Wiens
Interior design: Heimat House
Author photo: Andrew Vaughan

Represented in Canada by the Literary Press Group.

Distributed in Canada by the University of Toronto Press and in the U.S. by
Small Press Distribution (SPD).

The publisher gratefully acknowledges the financial assistance of the Canada
Council for the Arts, the Canada Book Fund, and the Province of British
Columbia through the B.C. Arts Council and the Book Publishing Tax Credit.

Printed and bound in Canada.

To Poppy,
whose stories I already miss

Acknowledgements

I would like to thank Anvil Press for giving these stories a home together. Many of them previously appeared in Canadian literary journals—from Vancouver to Fredericton—but were, until Brian Kaufman decided to pull them together, still living apart. I am delighted with the way this collection has ended up, impeccably edited with a brilliant cover that makes me smile.

"Maurice," the story of a bad-tempered dwarf from Prince Edward Island, appeared in *subTerrain* and caught the attention of Brian. That started this book. *Maurice* grew out of a story that my father, who was born in Charlottetown, told me, a story that was, like all of his fantastic tales, part fact and part fiction. I lost my father, Tom, during the editing of this book, but his spirit, humour, and some of his stories can be found in these pages. "Doll and Snooks" is a nod to his decades in the world of boxing.

My father told me that he liked me best when I was able to find the humour in life's dark moments. It took away the sting. Many of the stories in this book attempt to do that, to gently mock ourselves and the moments that could otherwise crush us, to start the healing.

Some of these stories were published in Canadian literary journals. "Valery the Great" and "The Favourite Nephew," *Other Voices*; "Maurice," "Bittersweet Bratislava," *subTerrain*; "Little Eric" *The Fiddlehead*; "I Visited the Grand Canyon," *Room*; "Bad Boys," *Pottersfield Portfolio*; "Hank Williams Is Coming to Save Us," *Qwerty*; "The Houdini," *The Dalhousie Review*; "A Great Nation," *Front & Centre*; "Freud's Rat Man Was Conflicted," *The Puritan*. Thank you to those editors.

My children, Hannah and Paddy, inspire me. I thank them and my husband, Andrew, for enduring the constant humming that accompanies my writing.

I am most grateful to the Nova Scotia Department of Tourism, Culture and Heritage for its continued financial support of me and other writers who would not otherwise be able to do this work. Thank you.

Contents

The Favourite Nephew

Floyd Barkhouse was a devotee of Western pulps, particularly those involving shootouts and prostitutes, and he patterned his writing on the more flowery authors. Floyd loved morality tales in spectacular settings. Heroes. Cowboys. Civil War veterans and stallions. He loved the feel of a paperback tucked in his back pocket like an overflowing wallet.

When Floyd approached his home computer, he breathed in deeply, the smell of cordite and cheap perfume flooding his nostrils, the sound of hoofbeats in his ears. As media liaison for the Wahoo Volunteer Search and Rescue Team, Floyd had to pump out releases the moment his team was activated: dramatic releases that invariably, and without a sniff of restraint, portrayed the team in the most heroic light.

"Sixty dedicated Wahoo members are combing the dense, dark woods outside Myrtle, N.S., for a ninety-year-old woman lost in the frosty moonstruck night. Teams of twenty men spreading out. Searchers. First aid workers. Saviours, we hope."

Floyd worked from the garage of his house, which he had converted into the team's communications headquarters. On the walls were maps and aerial photographs of the Wahoo area, an inland abyss of trees and back roads miles from the coastline. Instead of schooners and whale-watching, Wahoo had dirt bikes and tractors. Deer strapped to roofs. Men with a guaranteed twenty-minute response time ready to leap into action.

"Got any searches?"

Floyd looked up to see Kenny, his neighbour, in his doorway.

"Not yet," admitted Floyd.

Kenny was wearing a scarf from the thrift shop. On one side, it said: *Nova Scotia Power, Hurricane Juan 2003*, as though it were marking a fabulous success instead of a disastrous blackout that lasted for a full ten days. Over two-hundred-and-fifty pounds, Kenny measured five feet five from the soles of his moccasins to the top of his Boston Bruins toque. He had asthma.

"I'm goin' to da Buyway tomorrow."

"I reckon that's a good idea, Kenny. I reckon that's good."

Each November 1, Kenny lined up outside Buyway to purchase leftover Halloween candy at half price. Kenny, who lived with his mother, drifted about Wahoo, unrestrained by a real job or social expectations. The only place off-limits was the liquor store. One day, a clerk had sold Kenny a bottle of Captain Morgan, which he immediately consumed, only to vanish for twenty hours until he turned up under a playground slide with no recollection of how he got there.

"People like him can't drink alcohol," Kenny's mother explained. "He knows that, but he was in a state with Princess Di's death and all that. Kenny Stubbert loved Lady Di, you know. He absolutely loved her."

Short and rotund, Floyd looked as though his pants were hoisted up too high, unable to find a waistline. He wore a moustache, and when he donned his ball cap and aviators, he resembled a bank robbery suspect caught by surveillance cameras—disguised, but near recognizable.

The moment the alarm was sounded, Floyd's face would shift,

change in an indescribable way. What was different? People would wonder, staring at his duplicitous nose and mouth. And then, you could see *it* setting into his eyes, as plain as a cataract, the thirst for something catastrophic that would set him into action. Planning, moving, a disaster junkie feeding off strife.

Floyd filed an old release in his cabinet and then turned to Kenny, who had bristly grey stubble on his chin.

"How long you t'ink it'll be?" Kenny inquired.

"If I knew that, Kenny, I'd be God."

Every night when Floyd went to bed, he prayed that someone would get lost in the woods. Confused, disoriented, dehydrated, or near hypothermic—the details didn't matter, as long as they were *lost*. It wasn't just the excitement of writing his releases; it was a matter of keeping the rescue team alive with handouts from a beholden public. Most donations came in short bursts following a well-publicized rescue, spiking if a child or a senior were involved.

"Tonight, a four-year-old boy remains lost in the woods of Wahoo County. Thick, soggy woods, as unforgiving as a posse of vigilantes with the vile taste of murder in their mouths. Combing those woods is the Wahoo Rescue Team."

— 30 —

Floyd's extravagant releases did not diminish the good that the Wahoo rescuers did. In the past year, they had found the four-year-old boy, two hunters, one snowmobiler, a birdwatcher, and a long-haul trucker who had wandered into the bush during a diabetic episode. As soon as the truck had been discovered, Floyd had alerted the local TV correspondent, an affable fellow named Al, who worked from his basement.

"Bring out the cameras!" Floyd ordered Al. "We got a live one." And then ominously, over the speakerphone: "For now."

By midnight, the search had reached Stage Two, with a coffee station and floodlights. A converted school bus—the mobile command post—was painted fluorescent orange. And then, the glorious rescue captured by Al on his handheld video camera.

Floyd's bungalow was across the street from a gas station. In the station parking lot were wrecks, a tow truck, and a Buick LeSabre with two dead animals spread across the hood. *Lovely Fresh Rabbits*, said the handwritten sign. Floyd watched a Ford Ranger with a handicapped plate pull up. The driver jumped out, cradling a beer can covered with red electrical tape. It was Floyd's brother, Buddy. At the gas pumps, Buddy lit a smoke and hopped up and down as though he were on hot pavement.

Floyd kept his eye on Buddy. When Floyd was twelve, their mother sent him to live with his aunt Louise in Myrtle, and in retrospect, it was probably the best year of Floyd's childhood. He had his own room away from the incorrigible Buddy. Louise, a spinster who ran the post office, gave him his first pulp Westerns. The covers were as bright as a movie poster; the men were virile and toted guns; the women were buxom and squeezed into low-cut dresses. In the evening, in the shadow of dusk, the pair would sit in the den with their books: Floyd galloped across the Wild West on a pinto, and Louise made her way through English moors, besotted by Gothic love.

Aunt Louise's house had a duck pond and crabapple trees. But what made it magical was Babe, a miniature horse she had inherited from her brother, a farmer from Prince Edward Island. Babe was three feet tall and the colour of toffee. He could pull a tiny wagon or carry a child.

"Wahoo Rescue, Floyd." He answered the phone, and then replaced it, disappointed. When he looked across the street, Buddy was gone.

❀   ❀   ❀

Day twenty-seven without a search. The air was too quiet, too still, as though henchmen were rustling cattle from the local widow. Floyd heard branches crack and a sorrel gelding whinny. He opened a file on his computer. To maintain the team's presence in the public psyche, Floyd had begun writing vociferous letters to the weekly newspaper on a range of subjects: jaywalkers, bicycle helmets, waterslides. He always signed on behalf of the Wahoo team.

Dear Editor:

On August 17, I was alarmed to see in your newspaper a photograph of two teenage boys riding bicycles to Moss Creek Pond. Neither bicycle was equipped with a bell. I encourage you not to run irresponsible photos like this.

Sincerely Floyd Barkhouse, Wahoo Rescue Team

The paper's editor never questioned Floyd's expertise or his interest in the subject because Floyd consistently came down on the side of safety. Floyd understood safety from a number of perspectives. He had been a foreman at the poultry plant for twenty-seven years; in one of those queer coincidences, he had helped locate a silent gas leak at the plant on the same day that Treena, his wife, left without a word.

Floyd watched two kids tear by on dirt bikes spitting gravel, heading past the gas station that advertised *Ten-Year Anniversary Special: Kool Air slushies 25% off.* He saw a beater with Snap-on carseat covers and two tires in the backseat. It made him think about Buddy, who wore cowboy boots and Levi's topped with black

T-shirts displaying logos for motorcycles or tequila. Buddy was one of those lanky, hard-drinking types who always had a pack of smokes in his pocket, the type you could never imagine with a family or a pension. For some reason, Floyd's mother insisted, despite all evidence to the contrary, that Buddy resembled Audie Murphy, the fifties movie star, the most decorated veteran of World War Two, the wholesome American hero who had starred in Westerns. If, Floyd used to mutter, by Audie Murphy, you mean a shiftless bum who crashes cars, starts grease fires at 3 a.m., and sucker punches the opposing catcher at the end of a softball game.

It was no wonder, Floyd decided, that when he visited Aunt Louise in the nursing home, she pulled him close and, in a rare moment of lucidity, whispered: "I know your mother loves Buddy most, but you are my favourite nephew." Floyd had smiled.

Day thirty-six without a search. The Wahoo team conducted a simulated rescue. Floyd's team captain lectured trainees on how to put together a twenty-four-hour bag. He showed them the mandatory equipment, including a whistle, compass, and folding knife, as well as optional accessories such as bug repellent.

Floyd notified Al about the simulation. Al showed up, and ran a clip of Kenny, used in place of a dummy, being carried off in a basket stretcher. Kenny was in high spirits that day. He was wearing the official Wyatt Earp Collector Knife from Franklin Mint, a birthday present from his mother. He scratched his head and muttered something about fleas. Suddenly, Floyd could see Kenny, fat and foolish as a kitten, rolling in grass, a euphoric grin on his Cheezies-stained face, grass on his knife, grass on his duct-taped glasses.

At the end of the exercise, the skies erupted, soaking Al, the reporter, and the thirty volunteers. "This is nothing," Floyd said, his face as impassive as the innocent outlaw who had just outdrawn a bounty hunter. "This is business."

The next day, Floyd was watching television in his den, which was decorated with a moose head and photos of the rescue team meeting politicians. He saw a program about a blind man who used a miniature horse as his guide animal. Miniature horses were great guides, the program explained, because they had almost three-hundred-and-sixty degrees of vision, they lived forty years, and they possessed a docile nature. It made him think about Babe and Aunt Louise, who barely recognized him now, stricken as she was with Alzheimer's.

During the rescue team's last dry spell—forty-nine days without a search—Floyd visited Aunt Louise at the nursing home. When he arrived, the television was on a wedding channel. A girl who worked in a drive-through restaurant told viewers that her boyfriend had proposed, but she had turned him down until he returned with a ring of her liking. "I have very particular tastes," she said. "I like sapphires." The camera panned to the potential fiancé, who nodded his assent.

The floor nurse, a nervous girl from the city, scurried from the room. And then Floyd made one of those decisions that people never remember making, like slipping a pack of gum in their purse at the grocery store or drifting through a railway crossing in their car.

Aunt Louise flinched when the frosty air struck her face, Floyd recalled with a pang of guilt. He had given her ice cream—butterscotch ripple, her favourite—and bundled her up. She was wearing sneakers and a wool sweater with buttons. Floyd walked Louise five hundred metres behind the home, into the bushes near a patch of wild berries, and then stopped. "Look, Auntie Louise," he said, smiling. "I see Babe; he's hiding behind that tree."

"Oh Babe," Louise sighed and headed off.

"Yes, Auntie. I think he's sad."

At the time, Floyd wasn't thinking about Babe or Louise; he

was thinking about a story by James M. Cunningham, the story of a stoic marshal forced to take on a gang of outlaws, to risk the love of his Quaker wife for a thankless town. It wasn't the marshal's fault that no one had the guts to back him. It wasn't Floyd's fault that no one gave a damn about the rescue team until someone was lost. It was *High Noon* and he was Gary Cooper, a man too proud to run.

After the nurse reported Louise missing, the alarm went off, and then there was a parking lot full of lights. Buses. And in the woods, dozens of men beating through bushes, tying plastic tags onto tree branches, showing where they'd already been. It was as thrilling as leaping on the back of a blue roan Appaloosa without touching the irons.

The plan almost ended in disaster when Louise, proving to be more spry than Floyd had imagined a one-hundred-pound senior could be, covered three kilometres on foot. When they found her, she was resting in a patch of bull thistles. Aunt Louise, Floyd remembered far too late, had always been nimble.

The little nurse suspected that Floyd had planted Louise in the woods, but she was, quite frankly, nervous around the Wahoo search people, who had guns and ATVs and a queer look in their eyes. They were moose hunters and rabbit trappers, the side of Canadiana that city dwellers could not understand. The anti-gun-control people. The people with satellite dishes and mud-covered trucks. Big dogs that lived outdoors all year. The true Two Solitudes that divided the nation.

With admirable modesty, Louis L'Amour, author of more than one hundred books with sales of more than two hundred million, said he wanted to be remembered "as a good storyteller." Floyd wanted more. He wanted respect and admiration and some small claim to immortality. Wearing his ball cap and aviators, Floyd placed the Captain Morgan on the seat of his truck and headed out. It was hard to tell how far Floyd would take Kenny into the dense woods. At least Kenny, with all of his weight and all of his ailments, wouldn't be as nimble as Aunt Louise.

At the fire hall, Floyd saw a sign advertising a variety show with coffee and a light lunch. The admission was four dollars, he noted, with proceeds going to the rescue team. He hoped the turnout would be good.

Maurice

Maurice and his family lived next door to us on the Island. They were all dwarves: the mother, the father, the two girls, and Maurice. The old man worked on the coal boats and their house was chockablock with miniature furniture. One day, Maurice came by and said he wanted me to lead his gang. I said, "Okay," and he said, "Good, I've got a .45." I told him: "I ain't goin' with you if you got a .45." So he said, "All right, I'll take my BB gun instead." Just then my younger brother, Butch, showed up wearin' one of them cotton dresses the Old Lady used to put him in. He was around six, covered with soot, with hair the colour of ginger taffy. Butch would follow me anywhere, so I slapped his head and said, "Get lost, Shorty."

Me and Maurice looped Dizzy Square like G-men. There weren't much to see: a travellin' salesman haulin' pots, a farmer pickin' up labourers for four bits a day. Just when we figured we'd be better off at the track fillin' water buckets for the horses, Maurice spotted three nuns and got off a dandy shot. Spooked, they scattered like pigeons. One was the biddy who cuffed my ear when the Old Lady sent me beggin' for food when Butch was sick and the Old Man was down in the Maine lumber woods scrapin' for a buck.

I don't think Maurice hit 'em, just scared the meanness out of 'em, so I said, "Man, we better split. You ain't outrunnin' nobody, not even three old nuns, with *them* short legs."

After a week, Maurice was back like the peddle wagon.

"Sparky," he said, "I need your help with somethin'."

Maurice had a voice like a scrub board. I remember his eyes gettin' hard and starin' at somethin' I never could see. Maurice would talk and his eyes would widen like he was watchin' a movin' picture, a silent flick with Charlie Chaplin, but there weren't nothin' there.

He'd read a book, he said, and he had it aced. This Lebanese neighbour had a pig named Larry in his yard and Maurice was going to operate on him.

I said, "Count me out, man. I ain't operatin' on no pig."

When the war broke out, I joined the Navy, thinkin' I'd be a hero. They turned down Maurice, which made him feel pretty low, all washed up, like one of them old horses the farmers fed to the foxes. He started to hit the hooch and hang with the shakos. I heard he smashed a guy over the head with a two-by-four.

Around 1942, Maurice caught a break. He signed on a merchant ship with a bunch of Norwegians. Runnin' grub to the crew, helpin' Cookie, he was what they called a messman. Some guys fall apart after shit like that: duckin' subs, watchin' men die, but Maurice said it was good for his nerves, and at night, he slept like a Philadelphia lawyer.

After the war, Maurice moved to Norway with a woman he'd met on a flag tanker. She was a radio operator, a real tomato. They said Maurice opened an autobody shop. I don't know what kind of cars they had in Norway, but Maurice was sharp with his hands—he could fix anything. All my hands were good for was fightin', which was why I stayed in the game for fifty years: fighter, trainer, cut man.

A couple of years after the war, I was in downtown Halifax with Butch, who was tuned for a ten-rounder with Sailor Boy Doyle.

Butch had a bad hate-on for Sailor Boy, so I wanted to keep him on a short leash with his anger bottled up. Around midnight, we rolled into a clip joint that smelled like a card game and Minard's Liniment. Butch was feelin' pretty big in a double-breasted suit he'd bought with his last purse. Most of the time, Butch was whingy, but he looked sharp that night and he knew it. "Let's check 'er out," he said, noddin' to the back.

We made our way through the smoke, and who was playin' but the midget wrasslers in town for a show at The Forum. I loved to watch them perform. Man, they were agile. When The Little Beaver was young, he could cover the top rope like a squirrel. Sky Low Low could stand on his head with no hands for balance. Outside, they could be bad little buggers: one guy got caught pissin' out a hotel window; another liked to drink moonshine and yodel.

The Little Beaver was my favourite, naturally. They called him the King of the Midget Wrestlers. The papers said the Beaver was four foot four and weighed sixty pounds, but I thought he was bigger, the way he could lift a grown man or airplane-spin Sky Low Low. In my mind, Beaver was a better showman than Ali. Years later, I heard he died from emphysema in a little Quebec town.

Anyway, sittin' at the table with a dead man's hand was Maurice in a handwoven Panama with a pleated pearl ribbon. You'd have thought he was Howard Hughes, not some spud from the Island. I rubbed my eyes. "Maurice, what are you up to, man?"

"Sparky," he said. "I've gone into management."

Well, I let that pass. I was too busy lookin' at this tiger they had chained to the table, a full-grown animal with paws like hubcaps. Now, I seen tigers in South Africa when I had Rockabye Smith fightin' for the Commonwealth title, but this was a bit unusual.

We started talkin' and Maurice laid out some heavy shit he'd seen in the war: deaths, explosions, mutilations. He chucked her all in, bullshit chowder. Norway was as boring as the Island, he said, and they never done nothin' for the sailors after the war. I never asked about his wife; there was women there if you get my drift. I told him I got tin-fished in the English Channel but survived. Maurice laughed, which kind of insulted me, and when he did, that tiger's head shot up and snarled.

So the next time the midgets came to town, me and Butch went. I remember that night because Butch had fourteen stitches over his right eye; it was the same year that Marcel Cerdan was killed in a plane crash. Little Beaver was puttin' a hoofin' on Fuzzy Cupid and some big fool in the front row jumped up and screamed, "Beaver is an animal." Beaver was agile as a cat, but he weren't no animal.

When we went to the dressin' room, there was no sign of Maurice. He had split.

Years later, I had Archie Lucas down in New York for a six-rounder. Archie didn't have no papers and they held him at the border for ten hours on account o' him being black and quite possibly, in *their* minds, a Cuban hit man. Before it was over, Archie confessed to breakin' into the Legion at home and stealin' two dozen hams. Archie weren't ready for nothin' but a do-si-do, but we went to Gleason's and put on the gloves. When we came outside, Archie said he wanted a giant hot dog from the street vendor. I looked at Archie and said: "Man, you ain't gonna make weight as it is. You already ate them hams."

We hailed a cab and headed to our digs, Archie still jawin' about that goddamn hot dog. His brother, Jermaine, was the exact same way. The whole family had an awful weakness for cheap meat. Sittin' there, tryin' to ignore Archie, I looked at the driver's mug shot, and it seemed familiar despite the moustache.

"Man, I know you, don't I?"

The driver nodded. "Yeah, it's Maurice, brother. I'm a Neeeww Yawker now."

I told him to come to the fight on Friday night and we'd hook up after. He never did, or I never seen him, and that was that.

A few years back, my brother Butch got sick. They said it was from fightin', too many shots to the head like Ali, but I don't know. Butch liked to feint, to cover up. When Carmen Boucher fought him in New Brunswick, he said it was like tryin' to trap bubbles.

They put Butch in an old man's home on the Island, out in the country near some farms. I went to see Butch and it weren't that bad. The place was clean and Butch was out of it, jingle-brained. Someone had made a scrapbook of his clippings with a front page that said *"Island Boy Fights to Draw in Madison Square Garden,"* and they set it on his dresser for visitors to see, under his real name, Ralph. No one ever called him that except for his ex-wife, Katherine, and he screwed that up.

The nurses had big signs on everything. *Socks. Underwear. Today Is Harry's Birthday*. The place had that old-man smell, as musty as a root cellar. It was the guys who still knew what was happenin' that I felt bad for. One old guy was wearin' his service medals and talkin' about a 1928 Chevy he'd bought for a grand. Another guy kept drummin' the edge of the table with his fingertips. He was wearin' a trucker's hat and yellow-tinted aviator glasses, with the hat tilted down over one eye like a bad ass.

And then there was Maurice. After all he'd been through and all he'd seen, there he was, parked in a chair in a Habs robe and slippers.

Maurice seemed like somethin' out of a fairy tale. He was wearin' a porkpie hat and starin' out the window at a dusty clay road that looked like a roll of dried blood. It made me think of all the hand tapes I'd kept in a box, cut off and stained. After each fight, I added the name of the fighter and the date in ink, and they became records, really, of wins and losses, and wars that never shoulda been.

The nurse told me Maurice was having trouble with his legs and he couldn't walk right. He was real hateful to the other guys, she said. He'd call them washerwomen or ignorant spudheads.

I looked at Maurice and said, "What's happenin', man?"

He hauled himself up in his chair. Pretty soon, it all came out in that scrub-board voice. Maurice said that some years back, his wife, the tomato, took up with a skinny accountant who looked like Howdy Doody. They were skatin' around, meetin' in cars, makin' a monkey out of Maurice.

Maurice said he tried to shake it but it stuck in his shorts like sand, so he cut the brake lines to the guy's car. You know the end of that story: Howdy Doody in a wooden nightshirt.

An old farmer in wraparound sunglasses shouted, "They said they'd build a trout pond."

"*Gout?*" said his buddy. "Who the hell wants gout?"

Some hayseed with mud on his boots arrived to see an old-timer named Berle. His shirt was open to the waist like a flamenco dancer; his workboots were untied. He wore his hair in a style from the fifties, short on the sides with a greasy slip in front. His eyes looked half-crazy.

"Look at that fuckin' rhubarb," Maurice cursed out loud.

I looked at Maurice and shook my head. He had a rubber ball in his hand that he kept squeezin' like he was pumpin' blood to his heart over and over to keep himself alive. Maurice was always cool as ice, shootin' nuns or cuttin' up pigs, but I could tell by the way he was squeezin' that ball that it weren't all right.

I never had much brains to work with, but I know that life is a card game. At some point, your luck runs out. The cute moves, the clever shit, it all gets old. Stanley Ketchel, the Michigan Assassin, got himself shot to death at twenty-four for being a wiseass. Men, you see, always believe they're gettin' away with it: the missed anniversaries, the jackass excuses. It's like gettin' a paycheque with no taxes taken off. Somehow, they think the dough is theirs and no one will come lookin', but they are wrong because women are the most unforgivin' tax collectors on Earth. Women keep track of every nickel, every dime of deceit, and women are just waitin' to collect. Probably when the kids are grown or the house is paid. Then it will all come down: every hurt, every grudge, as bad as the goddamn Irish. And she may not leave in body, just in mind, movin' to a place she'd worked for, and it would be her place, not his, because he weren't never there to build it.

"You know, man," I said, because there were no moves left for me or him or Butch. "You're just tryin' to get through life and there are lunatics all along the way friggin' you up. No wonder I punched so many guys in the mouth. Half the bastards probably deserved it."

Maurice nodded like he'd heard it all before, and then he said, eyes as blank as a dead man's, "Amen, brother."

Little Eric

Ambrose vamped across the Delectable Donut shop. A swizzle stick of a man in a plum uniform and hat, he stopped at a matron's table and leaned into her space. "What are you looking at?" Ambrose widened his eyes extravagantly like a white-faced mime. "Not a flaw," he scolded. "It couldn't be a flaw, honey, because I'm flawless."

She giggled. Ambrose bussed a retired couple on their blanched cheeks, and then lifted the man's HMCS Haida ball cap to rub a head that felt like an old wedding dress, satin and worn. With aplomb, Ambrose opened a Coke can and took a drink. *Ahhhhhh.* Mid-morning, and the shop was brimming with Muzak, cushioned sneakers, and World War Two tattoos of *Mother*.

Ambrose headed for a regular named Katherine. She always dressed to go out. Her hair was starched in place, and she was monochromatically lilac from her knit slacks to her jaunty Apache scarf. Cream pumps for punch.

"How are you?" Ambrose covered Katherine's hand with his.

Katherine was a confidante.

"Good, good, my granddaughter was here to visit." Katherine stared the self-steadying stare of the elderly. From her window seat, she could oversee her car, a beige boat with a vanity plate that boasted *A Touch of Class* over a pink rose.

"You deserve it."

Katherine's lips were painted cranberry and her brows were drawn as carefully as a surgical incision. A faded beauty, she reminded Ambrose of his grandmother, who kept her collection of costume jewellery in a chocolate box shaped like a heart. Chunky beads and clip-on earrings in saffron, red, and buttercup. Once a year, on her birthday, someone drove Nana two hours into St. John's to visit the Ladies Dress Shop. Ambrose went with her, and Edna, the old gal who folded frocks for forty years, fussed over the annual indulgence like Nana was going to the Oscars.

"Something wonderful is going to happen," said Ambrose.

"Is it the message?" Katherine asked.

"Oh yes."

Katherine was always alone, and she bristled around the couples who flaunted their coupledom, the pairs who dressed alike and melded into one gender, nondescript people who had never been like her and Ralph.

"Don't get too excited," warned Katherine, who had learned to keep her heart protected like a rose bush, mulched with straw in winter. "You don't know with people."

Ambrose lived above a convenience store three blocks away. He saved his tips in a box labelled *Travel*, and twice a year, he took a shopping trip to Sainte-Catherine Street in Montreal, or once, for his thirtieth birthday, to New York City, where he saw Robert De Niro. Ambrose scooted across the shop to the sandwich-making area, where he picked up the disposable gloves and struggled, like OJ, to put them on.

"I was going to be a doctor," Ambrose deadpanned, "but I had trouble with the gloves."

"Ha ha," chuckled Hank, a veteran in an eye patch.

Katherine looked at Ambrose, and she saw—through the camp and bravado—a hunger that scared her, a yearning that could send you in all directions, bouncing off walls and landing with a thud. All Ambrose wanted was the same thing that she had wanted: the thing that could break your heart.

Ambrose came from a small village in Newfoundland. It had a fish plant and banks of drying nets. Wooden houses painted scarlet, blue, and yellow. Clotheslines. He and his brother, Gerry, had been exceptionally pretty children, blond with blue eyes and faces so exquisite that the old people were anxious around them, believing they would be snatched by faeries. When the sheoques, who were attracted to beauty, stole a child, they replaced him with a changeling who would die within a year. It was not good to look like Ambrose and Gerry, not good for anyone at all.

There were no coffee shops in the village, which had until 1966 been linked to the outside world only by boat. On the year that Ambrose turned twelve, the government gave the people a reward for voting Liberal: a restaurant run by "psychiatric survivors." It was the only brick building in the village, and it was low, with the squinty eyes of a women's prison. Inside were salt-resistant carpets and Arborite counters.

Ambrose attended the opening, which had pop and plastic bowls filled with potato chips for refreshment. "This is a great day for the town," proclaimed the local MP, who had descended from the heavens in a helicopter. "This is a great day for our community!"

The restaurant was named The Ocean View Diner. Soon, the workers dubbed it—with self-deprecating humour—the Ding-A-Ling Diner. For lunch, they made fish and chips and hot turkey sandwiches topped with peas. On Sunday, after church, they offered berry crumble and chocolate pie, which Ambrose, who lived nearby, helped serve. It was the first time some people had ever tasted coffee that was brewed, not instant.

Before long, people became friends with Clarence the cook, who sat on the back step during breaks, chewing tobacco while white mice ran relays inside his shirt. He had a favourite mouse named Little Eric. People gave Clarence wood shavings and nuts. Grateful, he put a little extra fish in the chowder.

❀   ❀   ❀

Ambrose had taken his semi-annual trip to Montreal a week earlier. Two days after he returned, he received a Facebook message from a person he did not know.

Hi. I saw you on the flight to Halifax. We didn't actually meet but there was something about you. I will be in Halifax and would like to get together.

There *was* something about Ambrose, something you could still notice from afar. While he had grown bony and haggard, his pants sagged, and he had lost some of his hair, his face, the same face that had discomforted the old people in his village, was in the right light, exquisite.

Since the email, Ambrose had been thinking about the flight to Halifax, which had started curiously when a basketball team shuffled on. A teenage boy was spinning a ball and wearing a Raptors jersey; another was squirming in a navy blazer. Some older men, coaches, looked smug at the convergence of youth and height, as though they had something up on everyone.

A boy squeezed into the seat behind Ambrose.

"How old are you?" Ambrose heard the flight attendant ask.

"Fifteen."

"Then, you'll have to move. Under federal regulations, you have to be sixteen to sit next to the emergency exit doors."

"But it's the only place I fit. I'm six eleven."

The boy sighed and his teammates laughed at his dilemma. By now, the other passengers were listening, intrigued by the possibility of a teenage giant in their midst.

"I'll move you up front," the attendant said.

The boy unfolded, a human tent, and an old lady gasped, "Oh

my!" He *was* almost seven feet tall, and his head bussed the ceiling. Dark, he had coarse features that seemed part of an endocrine syndrome, the imposing features of a James Bond villain with metal teeth. His face was at odds with his youthful vulnerability, and he lumbered forward, too tall, but too young to be entrusted with lives, a situation his teammates found hilarious.

Ambrose returned to his novel until the attendant, a man with brown eyes, a man who reminded Ambrose of Johnny Depp, began his pre-flight demonstration. He looked fun, Ambrose decided, like he packed tour books and time off for warm destinations. Ambrose could picture him in a Catalan farming village with narrow streets and open windows, tucked in the foothills of the Sierra de Cardo. Dale, Ambrose decided. His name was Dale.

After he started the demonstration, Dale realized that the ballplayers, intoxicated by their trip and the giant's predicament, found every move ridiculous. He pointed to the exits; they laughed. He tapped the overhead compartments, they snorted, infecting others. As the recorded instructions droned on, Dale braced himself. By the time he lifted the oxygen mask, he was trembling, trying to keep from laughing, and when he strapped the mask to his face, the cabin exploded like an apple in a microwave. A soldier clutched his chest as though he were having a heart attack; a hippie with a bag of cherries choked on a pit. Tear-stained, Dale forged through the pandemonium, and when he made his final gesture, the laughter became applause.

The rest of the flight buzzed with a happy familiarity. The ballplayers snapped digital photos of the Atlantic through their windows, and Dale, the good sport, strapped himself into a seat, facing back. Ambrose caught his eye and they shared a smile.

To Ambrose, the Ding-A-Ling was a haven from grief and second-hand clothes that smelled like mothballs. It had twelve square tables and flinty chairs. A wooden coat rack and a glass pie case. The manager gave Ambrose, who lived one street away, odd jobs, as well as leftover desserts which he took home to share. All of the workers moved too slowly, careful not to ruin the sanctity of their space. They washed the placemats by hand; they covered the canned milk with plastic wrap. They were stubbornly deliberate as though any departure from the blueprint could be fatal.

In the summer, when tourists tumbled into town, Ambrose picked daisies and flat-faced pasture roses with thorny stems and placed them on the tables. One day, after Ambrose arrived with an armload of fireweed, Clarence told him to watch himself around Mildred. The night waitress had a mean streak and had, many years earlier, in a dispute over a Polaroid camera, broken her brother's arm.

Ambrose had replied to the Facebook message:

That flight was a hoot. At the moment, I work at Delectable Donuts on Main Street until 5 on weekdays. I am in career transition.

And then: *Perfect. I'll drop by on Thursday at 5:00.*

CU then, Ambrose messaged back. *I'll be wearing plum.*

Clarence, the cook, had the round, soft-featured face of a celebrity chef; a man who could lose himself in demi-glace and bernaise sauce. His eyes twinkled and his mouth curled as if to say, "not bad." Before his illness, Clarence had owned a photography studio. Back then, he wore a double-breasted overcoat and a plaid scarf draped around his neck with panache.

One day, after the supper rush had ended, Clarence showed Ambrose a book of family portraits, the mainstay of his old business.

Clarence had posed the families in front of mantles. On beaches. Lying on hardwood floors, with the wife and kids gaily tossed upon the father like cushions. For variety, he used the same pose in snow or fall leaves. In one shot, everyone wore the matching blue jump-suits of garbagemen; in another, all five wore Irish knit sweaters.

After a while, Clarence realized that all of the poses—among trees, on beaches, in dining rooms—were disturbing. No matter how he posed them, someone was always up too high, and it made him believe, despite everything he knew, that the person was dead: the family ghost, the hovering saint. When they found Clarence, he was lying in a snowbank, crying so hard he could not stop.

Thursday, 4 p.m.

A teen in a one-shouldered top hustled through the Delectable door, brows plucked to a mean line.

"Dat bitch been hittin' up Shamar on his cellphone," she told her sidekick loud enough for others to hear. "Tellin' him they gotta chill."

The girls were waiting to use the washroom.

"What Shamar say?"

"He say he be at bingo wit' his mom."

"Shamar so comical."

The teen with the mean brows entered the washroom, and her friend, not knowing what to do, pulled out her cellphone and held it up, proof that someone, somewhere loved her. The air around her bristled.

Ambrose emerged from the kitchen, carrying a tray of donuts. He ignored the angry girl and turned to a taxi driver named Earl, who had a travel mug.

"Give me that mug, darling. Let me give it a good scrub."

The girls departed, slamming the door in the face of a senior. "What's the chance of getting a free coffee?" asked Earl, playful.

"Pigs may fly, but they are very unlikely birds."

"Who are you calling a pig?" jousted Earl, plump and pink as Spam.

"Not you, sweetheart. You're a tiger."

Ambrose's uncle, Spurgeon, helped build the Ding-A-Ling. He was a carpenter who wore overalls and a plaid shirt covered with sawdust. Spurgeon spoke in a slow cadence that reminded Ambrose of a dream he often had. In the dream, he and his brother were in a rowboat. The fog had burned off like taffy and the sea was asleep. Someone had given them each a quarter for ice cream, and they laughed and sang and counted strokes out loud. Skirting jellyfish, they rowed past Malcolm House's lobster pots, past a one-room schoolhouse with a pot-bellied stove. They bowed their heads at a graveyard they visited on Sundays, leaving daisies for poor souls lost at sea. At a point of land near the general store, they hauled up their boat. "Two ice cream cones," Ambrose pronounced, "one vanilla and a strawberry for my brother. Yes, he is growing tall; he's drinking lots of milk." They dipped their hands in the water to clean them of ice cream, and there was no need to talk when they resumed rowing, trading off with sore, wet hands. Ambrose nodded at puffins and a northern gannet; his brother nodded back, head as white and woolly as a cloud.

One day, Spurgeon arrived at Nana's house with a coffin.

"Do you like it?" he asked, picking a callus from his thumb, as though he were peeling a hard-boiled egg.

"Oh my Lord!" Tears filled Nana's eyes. "I've never seen anything so fine."

Nana had Spurgeon place the maple coffin in the living room

in a spot where the afternoon sun struck, beams of rejuvenating light that soothed Nana's nerves and zapped the airborne twitches. She covered the coffin with a crocheted doily.

After Spurgeon left, she summoned Ambrose. Look closely, she instructed him. It is solid maple, one-hundred-fifty board feet. Grander, she explained, than anything she had seen growing up in a plain board house built with the sweat of men who worked too hard for far too little, men like Father who hand-lined from a dory. "See how the grain flows," she whispered. "See, dear, see. You and I are the only ones who know something nice."

Nana lifted the lid and climbed inside. Arms folded, she rested, head raised on a pink pillow. *Mmmmmmm.* Ambrose did *not* want to look. He did *not* want to see it. *This* is how I should be laid out, she told him, in the wrap dress with the Peter Pan collar, the one we bought last year at the Ladies Dress Shop. "You know the dress, Ambrose, the red one. We'll do this right this time, not like when your poor little brother died. God rest his soul."

Thursday, 4:45 p.m

Katherine had returned to the coffee shop. She was sitting at a window table, dressed in yellow, Ralph's favourite colour. When she met Ralph—she never called him Butch—she was a beauty queen, an actual beauty queen, who had ridden on a float with ladies-in-waiting. She wore a white dress and a crown. She had a beautiful voice and sometimes she sang at weddings. Maybe if Gerry hadn't died when Ambrose was ten, she thought, he would not have been afraid of his looks. Maybe he would have become a model or an actor; maybe he would have not worked in a coffee shop, where customers, even the ones who loved him, wondered: Why can't he do something more?

Ambrose checked his watch, and then brightened as two party dolls rumbled up in an Oldsmobile '98 with a plate that warned: *Here Comes Trouble*. Bleached blonds, they teetered into the shop in high heels and strained jeans that could barely contain them.

"Two double doubles," one rasped through a filter of Export A.

"It's Margie's birthday," the other informed Ambrose. "We're going to celebrate tonight."

"Downtown?"

"That new country bar."

"I hear it's great. How old, Margie?"

"I'm twenty-six."

"Yeah and I'm Amelia Earhart. Call off the search."

The party dolls cackled and coughed up phlegm.

In the parking lot, the angry girls had returned with a familiar posse. One boy was wearing Exco jeans cut off like pedal-pushers and a ball cap tilted sideways as though he'd been smacked in the head. The boy pointed at Ambrose, who was clearing a window table. The boy pulled out his cellphone, read something from it, and laughed until his undersized head was red. My God, Katherine thought, what if it was them? The boy ape-walked by the window and grabbed his crotch. His posse howled approval.

Thursday, 4:55 p.m.

Ambrose bolted to the kitchen. When he returned, his hat was askew, and then, before the spot in his chest could tighten like the confines of a coffin, Ambrose closed his eyes and imagined himself someplace warm. When Ambrose opened his eyes, Hank was standing before him in welding-strength sunglasses.

"Chantelle said she'd save me a tin of mocha," said Hank. "It should be back there with my name on it."

Jeering, Exco boy pressed his face to the window, under a missing person's poster, over Katherine's seat, and licked the glass lasciviously. He had a unibrow and the small unpredictable eyes of a Japanese Akita, eyes you couldn't reason with or reach. He was wearing a bandana under his ball cap.

"This has been *such* a bad week," Ambrose sighed, turning his back to the baiting that seemed as pointless as the death of Little Eric. The restaurant had been preparing for a wedding reception, and Ambrose had arrived early with a fist of lady's slippers, delicate purple blossoms that appeared in May and were *never*, he was told, over and over again, to be picked. He'd picked them anyway, tired of buttercups and red clover, yearning, as he had all his life, for something lovely.

And then Mildred, the night waitress, ruined it all by throwing Little Eric in the fish chowder. She only did it to be vicious. Little Eric's death, Ambrose decided, was divine retribution for breaking a rule, a shitty rule that should *never* have applied to people like him and Clarence, people who could smell colours and taste pain, people with scars so fresh you could see them.

"It should be back there," Hank insisted.

Hands braced on the table, Katherine felt herself rising toward Ambrose and then she stopped. Ambrose shook a pile of napkins as though he were shaking out bugs.

"I'll come back when Chantelle is in." Hank shuffled off, and Ambrose looked at Katherine, who was wearing knee-high stockings that stopped, unbeknownst to her, two inches below her canary yellow skirt.

"It has been *such* a bad week," he sighed.

"Really?" Her rouge was garish slashes.

"A death in the family," Ambrose lied.

Katherine frowned at the splotches that were staining Ambrose's skin, spreading like the exploding dye from a bank heist. Why wasn't he more careful? she wondered. Why did he leave himself so open to hurt? It *always* happened. *Dear God,* muttered Katherine, who could not forget the day that she had collected the mail and found a letter about Ralph, *her* Ralph, from a woman named Lucille Carew.

"That's terrible," she mumbled.

"She was ninety-six and had a good life," blurted Ambrose.

The words poured out shamelessly, lifted from a book of clichés, and then, just as Hank put the run to the jeering teens, a taxi pulled into the parking lot, and a man with soft brown eyes bounded out.

Bad Boys

"I likes dat show Cops."

"It's all roight."

"I likes dat song dey play when dey're haulin' in da crooks in underdrawers, wit' dere eyes buggin' out of dere heads like a sculpin, and dey go: *'Bad Boys, Bad Boys, what you gonna do when dey comes for you?'*"

"Yeah, I likes that, too."

They cackled.

"I'd like to see dem come up here and do dat show."

"Me, too."

"Juss for somethin' different."

Lester and Lawson nodded as a woman shuffled by with a shopping cart full of kids. It was Thursday, and the aging strip mall in Wahoo was crawling with marginal shoppers looking for deals on toilet paper and no-name shampoo. Bags of marbles and paper plates. *High-end vinyl at low prices.*

"I'd like to see dem cops swoopin' in on Buddy's hair studio." Lester pointed across the strip mall at Classy Hair and Aesthetics. "And drag da bugger out, hair mussed, apron turned upside down, curlers spillin' on the floor, and dat music playing: *Bad Boys, Bad Boys...*"

Lawson savoured Lester's meanness; he soaked it up like the last swipe of gravy on a plate. Lawson studied the salon, decorated with 1950s photos of Sicilian playboys in pompadours, and nodded, "Dat would be good."

Lawson and Lester shared a bag of roasted-chicken chips, licking the salt from their fingers like dogs licking pavement. On cue, the salon door opened for a crisp man in a white shirt, who flicked his head sideways, relishing the saucy *click click click* of his heels on tile.

"Dey hauled up four in town last week," Lester said.

"Four dressers?" Lawson sounded excited.

"Ooooh yes, I seen it on TV. Cops say da buggers are breaking some Cosmopolitan Act."

"What's dat about?"

The two men stared at their shoes, seeking answers. Lester had duct-taped his Wallabees together while Lawson was wearing classic two-stripe sneakers with the sides slit for air. Lester picked up his story: "I dunno, but some of da dressers won't go for it. I seen one on TV."

"One of da dressers?"

"Ohhhh yessssss. No mistakin' dat. He was wearin' an orange flattop and he was roight hiss-terical, nearly out of his skull. Red Rooster, I called him, because of da way he was flappin' around."

They laughed like they were watching an Adam Sandler movie.

"I had a rooster once; it was roight vicious, bit da old lady." Lester looked around. "He shoulda killed her."

They laughed so hard that their eyes closed tight, leaving surface cracks in the fat.

"Well dis was juss a tiny little fella, probably a hunderd-twenty, soppin' wet. He said he's been doing hair since pageboys and crew cuts; dat he done Anne Murray once when she come through town. Of course, everybuddy says dat, roight? He said he was an artiste, and dat dem udder fellas wouldn't know a feather cut from a duck's ass. He even said he had another dresser down on Broadway who would vouch for him."

"Yeah?" asked Lawson, impressed.

Lester hauled out a smoke and lit it. A worn man humped a

pinball machine into Harry's Used Goods, a store that boasted toaster ovens and a singing bird clock that Lawson coveted. Lester nodded at the man and smiled.

"Juss from the way he said it, I t'ink he mighta been with *Cats*?"

"Yeah?" Lawson raised his brows, impressed.

"He never come out and said it, but dey got a lot of hair, roight, dem cats?"

"Oh yes, dats why dey're always choking on furballs."

Lester attempted a smoke ring. "I had one that near choked himself to death. Dem calicos is the worst, but I hates to part with them since dey're so pretty. So den the cop comes on, a big barrel-chested fourflusher, the kind dat would clip you wit' a sallywinder."

Lawson's eyes narrowed. "Probably didn't give a rat's ass about hair."

"Roight. He said some stoolie ratted out Red Rooster. Told da cops da Rooster was wearing a cape for dye jobs and permanits, and didn't have the proper papers to back it up."

"Yeah?" Lawson scowled. "Fookin' papers."

"Well, da Rooster said he juss liked dat cape; he juss liked to wear it."

"What's wrong with dat?"

Lawson tried to sound tough as Lester hobbled across the strip mall to pocket an empty Cola can. Lester stopped and stared at a bulletin board that offered babysitting services and eternal salvation. *On May 14, 1992 God spoke to me. The next round-up is sooner than you think. If people think I am crazy, I will go on national TV. I will submit to a lie-detector test. Society won't give me a chance.* He hobbled back.

"Dat poor little dresser, he looked like he was going to cry, runnin' on about Broadway and a double-o and a bandhouse clip. Roight pitiful, he was." He blew his nose into a hankie, and picked up his crossing-guard sign; Lawson's was still on the ground. "Still, I'd like to see dem on TV."

They stared across the mall at Harry's Used Goods and Roma's Dollar Store, and Lawson sighed, as long and sad as a loon, "Juss for somethin' different."

Valery the Great

I had never seen a bear on skates: four hundred pounds of shaggy fur and muscle, as powerful as fate, as incongruous as a flying pig.

When I first saw Valery in a cavernous rink, four thousand miles from home, I squinted to study his long snout and covered feet. I felt a peculiar sense of optimism as though the world were larger and more mysterious than I had imagined, grand enough to absorb my pain like sand swallowed by the sea.

Upright, with a hockey stick and helmet, the bear moved across the ice, diminished by the cold muffled space. A blond man was directing him. Both were in training attire, a track suit for the man and a collar for Valery. Satisfied, the man gestured toward the boards, and a woman guided a second bear onto the surface.

"Take your time, Vladislav," the man shouted in Russian.

"He is a bit tired," apologized the woman.

The second bear seemed tentative, less proficient. He held up his broad paws—shaped like catcher's mitts—as if he was going to swat at something. I imagined bears in their natural habitat, dens with beds of dry vegetation, earthy and organic, unlike the fabricated rink. As the woman emptied a bag of hockey pucks, I studied the bears' skates: moulded plastic with three buckles each.

Silent, I watched until it was time for me to go to the dressing room, where I, in a ritual I had followed for twenty years, laced up my skates. I thought about the bears, circus staples for centuries, creatures with frightening strength and an inexplicable allure, and wondered what would Mother think. Would she share my relief, the lightening of our burden?

I remembered the day Mother bought my first skates, leather and impossibly white, the transcendent white of angels. Unlike hockey skates, they had inch-high heels, and they came in a cardboard box, which I kept, like everything from that time, for fear it would be taken.

In Mother's mind, I would become ethereal, swathed in layers of tulle, as glamorous as Pavlova. I would hover on a cushion of greatness. That did not transpire, but I did find myself in Moscow years later with the Russian Circus on Ice and two skating bears. Valery and Vladislav are Eurasian brown bears—members of a species known as *Ursus arctos*—and distant relatives of the feared grizzly. They can execute slapshots with the accuracy of a sniper.

On the day my mother bought my skates, I saw a man riding a bicycle with a cat draped over his shoulder like a fly plaid. Pinned, prone, an impossibly inert mound of fur and flesh.

"Is that a Norwegian forest cat?" asked my mother.

I cringed, hating Mother's forced way with strangers.

"No," the man replied, eyes as vague as euphemisms. "It's a Maine coon cat."

Hours later, I saw a man driving an Eldorado with a bear strapped on the roof like a moving-day mattress. Tied, prone, an impossibly inert mound of claws and teeth.

"Is that a brown bear?" asked Mother.

"No," the man replied. "It's black."

That night, I saw a woman skipping down the road kicking her heels and playing a woodwind, eyes as wild as partridge berries.

"Is that a flute?" Mother asked.

"No, it's a piccolo. Would you like to try?"

"Sure," said Mother, nodding. She took the piccolo and touched, because she had to, something new. I watched motionless, enclosed in a shell of vulnerability, while Mother thrashed through the undertow of our grief. "It's very light," she said with an interest that seemed sadly strained. I nodded, seeing a pristine room, a trajectory of chances. When Mother turned, her eyes were filled with a sorrow that defined us, a sorrow that told us that, in our damaged state, we needed something hopeful to fill Father's place, something as mundane as a pair of skates.

My mother, Eleni, was beautiful with a regal neck and blue eyes that looked perpetually curious. In Russia, she had been a *feldsher*, or medical aide, who dispensed home remedies including dough plasters soaked in honey and rye. Before my father was killed, she filled our home with the smell of Siberian dumplings and potato pancakes. Afterwards, when joy had given way to vigilance, Mother made beet soup and bread. Each day, she walked me to my school where the janitor, sensing our delicate state, greeted her in the same heartening way.

"You lose weight?" Barney would inquire.

"Well, a bit, actually," Mother nodded, intent on stripping down our lives to the ascetic core.

"You look some healthy."

Barney spoke with authority on all health matters. He was a survivor of a frightful form of cancer, a struggle that defined him. Barney spent most of his days chatting up mothers or trading running tips with befuddled fathers. Never in a hurry, never too busy to chat. "Mr. Fowler wanted to paint the lobby." Barney would fold his arms across his chest. "I told him that might interfere with the talent show."

Burly enough to spin boys over his head with one arm, Barney seemed a valuable ally. "That little one is going to be in the Olympics some day," Barney predicted. "I can tell by her determination. You'll see."

It was clear that Dimitri favoured Valery.

The bear was special, he explained, endowed with rare gifts. Dimitri had named him after the godlike Valery Kharlamov, a legend of Soviet hockey, the golden boy of the golden era. Kharlamov, a mere five foot eight, had dazzling skating and stickhandling skills that belied his stature, moves as unpredictable as Nijinsky's.

"It is an honour for this performer to wear the Number 17," Dimitri would explain while putting on Valery's sweater. "Not anyone would be so respected."

Dimitri was protective of his Valery, reminding people the world is full of thugs and gangsters ready to prey on The Gifted. In that vein, he often mentioned Bobby Clarke, a name from the annals of Canadian hockey history. In one of the sport's more tawdry moments, the Flin Flon native had attacked Valery's namesake during the 1972 Summit Series. In desperation, at the turning point of a series compared to war, the toothless Canadian slashed Kharlamov's ankle, breaking it.

"Some people are made of silk," said Dimitri, grouping Valery with the hockey idol and Nijinsky, who eventually succumbed to mental illness. "Others, of burlap. Maybe, the burlap can endure more, but is it beautiful? Is it special?"

Vladislav, the second bear, was named after the incomparable Tretiak and wore the goaltender's Number 20. Dimitri had both of their hockey sweaters sewn by Raisa, the costume maker. Raisa could perform magic with fabric, forgoing patterns, sizing by sight alone, creating intricate swans, rag dolls, and gypsies. Raisa was quick. She once sewed, in a single day, twenty *kosovorotkas.*

Despite her talent, Raisa felt she was not given the same respect as the other artists, that she was looked upon as a tradesman. Burlap instead of silk. Because of this slight—real or imagined— Raisa made herself seem greedy and crude. If anything was up for grabs—a hotel room, an invitation to a reception—she would snatch it like she was grabbing the last of the *pelmini,* stuffing it into her face as though she might never see *pelmini* again.

Someone said that Raisa was the only child of elderly parents, conditioned to expect the extra treat, the gratuitous praise. "Spoiled girl," spat Yuri, the clown, when he arrived at breakfast to see Raisa trundling off with a pumpernickel. Raisa pretended that she did not care what others thought, but sometimes, she would grow maudlin and seek comfort from men. For a while she had been spending nights with the man who cleaned the animals' stalls, but that soon ended.

I spent my childhood in a New Brunswick city, a place with one Legion hall and a curling club, a place that choked on black air from a pulp mill. It had dentists who only did extractions and drifters who combed the streets for butts. It possessed a small tony end.

My family had never met the Bonangs until they joined Father's tennis club. She was an androgynous pharmacist with blotchy skin; Greg Bonang was a real estate dealer with close-set eyes and two cars: a BMW he drove to social gatherings and a decrepit Honda he piloted to the homes of widows. He would frequently be spotted in older neighbourhoods, trunk filled with *For Sale* signs.

Hovering between two genders, Belinda Bonang resembled a fifty-year-old man who had refused to age gracefully, the odd accessory at the sailing club. In a pea jacket and too-tight jeans, she walked with a curious strut, pushing from the back of her heels. She always seemed to be coming from a workout, though the incessant exercise did nothing to improve her appearance and instead made her more androgynous and blotchy.

Drawing an immutable line between Them and Us, she dropped constant references to private schools and stock options. On Father's salary as the tennis coach, we were clearly Thems. Ironically, she was forever on the lookout for someone who might be getting a deal that could, according to her calculations, be at her expense. When she joined the tennis club, she was outraged to learn that veterans received a discount. "Do you know that we are subsidizing them to the tune of ninety dollars a year?"

Whenever her husband entered the club, he looked like he was in a foreign country. He came from a coastal village known for the indiscriminate theft of cars, lobsters, and, on one occasion, a government boathouse. The Bonangs were unwieldy families of twelve or fourteen. They sometimes (without knowing it) married their cousins or, in rare cases, half siblings, producing a recognizable line of tiny children with close-set eyes. Sensitive about his background, she included him in her ostentatious boasts. "We just got back from Tuscany," she would sigh. "Greg wants to move there. I said, 'Give it a few years.'"

For all of the bragging, all of the spending, they remained an insignificant-looking couple whose house had a delusive feel. And then one day, when returning from a long lunch with a pharmaceutical salesman named Ernie, she drove her GMC Suburban over Father's bicycle and our small world collapsed.

In our house, despair weighed down upon my shoulders like an X-ray cape, a million pounds of leaden grief. The solution, I decided, was to retreat into the extreme quiet that would make me invisible, an untouchable target for savagery.

With a resilience forged in the cruel climate and harsh history of her homeland, Mother did the only thing she knew how to do: she adapted. She believed we could escape into a parallel world of death spirals and spins, an alternate life with a new language and impenetrable borders. "You will become, Maria, a wonderful skater."

Russia was a land of beauty and starkness, opulence and hardship.

I had visited once before with Mother, but that trip was focused on family. This time, on my own, I noticed stray dogs and protesters with costumes and signs. I was vaguely aware of ancient monasteries and underground dance clubs that, coldly, in the tradition of Club 54s, rejected people who didn't look hip. I saw kiosks selling vodka or flowers, but none of it touched me.

The circus world, like the one Mother and I had created years earlier, was snugly self-contained. With our own refrigerating system, we moved from town to town, welcomed as practitioners of Russia's most egalitarian art form. We had acrobats, gymnasts, doves, clowns, spinners, the air ring, jugglers, and trained dogs under the direction of Vera Kobolov, who dyed her poodles in pastel shades.

I was in the dance chorus. We performed a traditional Russian dance at the start of the show and a ballet-inspired piece at the end. With bolts of spandex and holographic knits, with sequins and tulle, Raisa transformed us into brilliant peasants and iridescent swans. Raisa was vain about her ability to size by sight, and we never had fittings, receiving our costumes complete.

Our choreographer was a woman named Anna, married to a contortionist from Mongolia. Like many artists, Anna was both blessed and cursed with sensitivity, an acute awareness of the sounds and thoughts around her. Something sad had happened to her, and, as a result, she seemed benumbed. I sensed her pain, the clawing fingers of injury that tear up your stomach like an ulcer.

One day during rehearsal, I saw Raisa brush by Anna.

"I don't know how she stands it," whispered a member of the chorus.

"Why?" I asked.

"After what she did with Anna's husband?"

"What?"

"Anna came home and found them in bed. When Anna told her to leave, Raisa refused, saying Anna's husband had promised her cake."

"Really?"

"Oh yes, it is always about her."

"Oh my."

"Everyone puts up with her because she is a genius with liquid lamé. Anna knows that, and I think that hurts the most."

Before I escaped to Russia, I was a pairs skater with a boy named Jeffrey. We went to the same high school, a ramshackle maze from the sixties, a wreck bereft of textbooks and washroom doors. It had water stains on the ceiling and holes punched in the walls, indignities we ignored, knowing our real lives existed outside school. One day during lunch, we walked across town for the funeral of a classmate, a boy we barely knew, an apparition. He lived in public housing, a ghetto of large dogs and so many murders that cops callously called it "a self-cleaning oven." He had fallen off a roof and died.

Jeffrey and I sat up front and turned as mourners arrived: a gang of awkward teens, men in windbreakers, girls who wailed like alley cats and then collapsed. Finally, an old woman hobbled in, crooked and bent, hair plastered to her skull like the pelt of an oily grey ferret.

Transfixed, Jeffrey stared. The woman was wearing a nylon coat with stains around the zipper. It groaned when she moved.

"It's the grandmother," someone whispered.

"Oh," nodded Jeffrey, who lived, like me, with his mother.

Her friends, two old women in matching attire, stopped for breath, clinging to a pew. Red-faced, one clutched her heart and looked up, beseeching. "Come here!" the grandmother cackled to the friend, who nodded her off, gasping: "Not yet, not until I get my breath." The grandmother patted the pew, insistent. She pulled her coat together and sniffed the air. Her friends settled into their seats, heads in like prehistoric turtles, but the grandmother fiddled. "It's cold in here, ain't it? Can't that old priest turn up the heat? The old bugger would squeeze a cent till the Queen cried."

"Oh my, oh my." She nudged the friends as the family arrived, sagging like tarps filled with rain. "I seen more meat on a hockey stick," she cackled, pointing at a distraught teen with the same face as our deceased classmate. And then, in a moment that chilled me, a moment that convinced me that life can be as cold and hard as a Siberian winter, the grandmother snorted: "Cry all you want. It won't bring him back. He's fly bait."

Jeffrey bolted from the pew and ran.

Yuri the clown drank too much.

He had a flat nose and brown eyes that drooped, giving him a mournful but comical look. For an entire week, he had participated in celebrations marking the sixtieth anniversary of Hitler's defeat: fireworks, parades, old war movies. One night, Yuri attended a performance by another circus. In the closing act, the director had monkeys portraying Nazis, later explaining that his first choice, the leopards, were too difficult to dress in uniform.

Yuri said the monkeys did a terrible job.

"What would you expect?" snipped Raisa. "They are only monkeys."

"That is no excuse," said Yuri. "They could have played the Nazis better. They were silly and childish. Dimitri's bears could have done a finer job."

"I would never put Valery in a Nazi costume," Dimitri snapped.

"Why?" Yuri taunted. "Are your bears too good for us?"

Dimitri lunged at the clown: "Drunken fool."

Raisa laughed though no one knew which side she was taking.

"At least I am not a barbarian," Yuri ducked Dimitri's charge.

"What are you talking about?" demanded Dimitri.

"Haven't you seen the letters? Animal activists are trying to put barbarians like you out of business. They are sending out bulletins."

"Bulletins?"

"About the cruel way you treat your animals."

Dimitri's face tightened. After Valery performed a difficult trick, the bear would press his face to Dimitri's as though receiving a kiss, a gesture that crowds loved. Was that cruelty? Barbarism? Dimitri followed the philosophy of the famed animal trainer Vladimir Leonidovich Durov, who stated, "Cruelty is humiliating. Only kindness can be wonderful." Watching Dimitri work with the large creatures, it was hard to believe that his brother, Andrei, a former strongman, was an enforcer with the mob.

"I will tell what a barbarian is," Dimitri spat. "A barbarian is a man like Bobby Clarke."

Each day, like shift workers, Jeffrey and I trudged to a rink near a strip mall.

The mall housed a liquor outlet and a dollar store where people in rubber boots and sweatpants could buy a bag of knick-knacks for six dollars. Someone was always on the phone, trying to locate another cashier, lost in an avalanche of Chinese trinkets and toiletries. Up front was a display of one-dollar reading glasses. I remember seeing a senior shuffle by an Easter display of chocolate rabbits. Nearby were potted plants made of cloth. "Oh, those white lilies," she groaned, clutching a ceramic dog with melancholy eyes. "They remind me of death."

Sometimes, Hilda, our coach, sent Jeffrey to the liquor store for gin. A doctor's wife, Hilda lived in a riverside mansion with a swimming pool and two Abyssinian cats. Years ago, she had appeared in the Ice Capades, a feat that had provided her with minor celebrity status and an unrelenting need for adulation.

Hilda had a childish nature that adults mistakenly believed gave her a rapport with young people. Jeffrey and I knew her petulant side, how she would snap if someone had forgotten her morning hot chocolate or her birthday. Like most teens, we lived in two worlds: the one parents saw, and the one we really inhabited; so we hid the truth, not wanting to disappoint our mothers, who felt proud knowing their children were being taught by such an esteemed figure.

Under Hilda's charge, Jeffrey and I followed a path as narrow as a laser beam, a path that precluded parties or after-school get-togethers. We spent our youths in a rink with rusty lights and infrared heaters dangling from the ceiling. An ice machine pulled by a tractor. At the entrance of our rink was a vending machine that produced a hockey card for a quarter. The card could, depending on your luck, feature Gretzky or Tie Domi. Like the Stoics, who traded sensual pleasure for spiritual bliss, the Hebrew sects who fasted to experience the holy, Jeffrey and I set our sights on a higher reward. One January, armed with bottles of water and fruit, we boarded a train to Montreal. Jeffrey placed a paperback on his seat where others could see it.

"It's a good read," he said. "I've read it probably four times."

I picked up the book: Albert Camus's *The Outsider*.

"I read it in French," Jeffrey added. "In French, it's called *L'Etranger*."

"You don't speak French."

Jeffrey shrugged. He was still at the age of self-deception and boundless hope. So, days later, he was stunned when during the long program, the favourites, a brother-and-sister pair from Aurora, fell three times and beat us. It wasn't the loss that did it; it wasn't the blow of watching the siblings grimace, then smile in relief. It was the sight of Hilda, tilting her head with a fake pout, meant it seemed to mock Jeffrey and me, the wretches who had handed her their faith. "They don't have the money, anyway," she told a matriarch in fur. "It takes talent and money to go all the way. *We* know that."

While Jeffrey cried, I froze in mortification. My past pain resurfaced like post-polio syndrome. As my vision faded and my feet went dead, all I could see was a crummy rink with a tractor, vagrants covered with mould, hockey thugs who sprayed shaving cream through the vents of Jeffrey's locker, soiling his clothes. It all seemed so tawdry—a bingo hall of dreams.

"How could that happen?" asked Mother, whose eyes looked short-circuited by the shock of being told that I, the essence of her life, did not matter.

"This is Pablo," Jeffrey announced weeks later. "He's visiting from Spain."

"Hello, Pablo." I looked at the stranger's sullen face.

Pablo had a jagged scar down one cheek; his teeth were as

stained as an old tablecloth. Jeffrey started to explain something about time off and a herniated disc, and then he stopped mid-sentence and chewed a cuticle over and over until he drew blood. Pablo's face hardened. Jeffrey's nervous state felt like a propane leak that had left the air unbearable, an explosive concentration of angst. I couldn't face the end of our dreams or the purple bruise that Jeffrey had covered with makeup, so I stared out the door at a drifter riding a bicycle, workboots unlaced, wearing a T-shirt that claimed *Everyone Looks Good at 2 a.m.*

Before the tsunami hit Sri Lanka, workers spotted antelopes heading for the hills; they saw elephants trumpeting and breaking chains. Flamingos left the lowlands and flew to the mountainous areas, but man does not, it seems, have the same prescient sense of danger. One night, Raisa secretly opened the door of Valery's cage and attempted to place a sailor's cap on his head, determining if it fit. The cap had one star and a floppy blue tassel. Valery, the most gifted of all the bears, a virtuoso named after the godlike Kharlamov, bit Raisa's arm off at the shoulder.

I Visited the Grand Canyon

There is no point in describing a man who traverses Nova Scotia on a ten-speed bike with a concertina strapped to his back, is there? Let's just say that Randy was resourceful, which is why he answered my ad in the first place.

"Hello," said a rural voice steeped in green work shirts and sea urchins. "Do you have an accordion for sale?"

"Yes, I do," I replied. "It's actually an English concertina with ebony ends."

"Does it have all the buttons?"

"Hmmmm, yes."

"Would you be willing to trade for a set of walrus tusks?"

"Yes," I said for no sound reason. "I guess so."

Randy arrived the next night from Mushaboom, winded, with the tusks. Short and wiry, he was wearing an army backpack and glasses that, through an optometrical misadventure, made one eye appear larger than the other.

I never would have met Randy if I had listened to my mother, who had warned me against placing the ad. "You will get *all kinds* of people," she cautioned, raising the spectre of axe murderers and religious fanatics. Randy, who was neither, was about to make the return trip when I paused. I admired his independence and his membership in an underclass of Maritimers who never bought anything new. People who purchased beds from Sally Ann, T-shirts emblazoned with empty boasts like *I Visited the Grand Canyon*, cutlery from a shop that displayed not only a Mexican sombrero, but a full-length prosthetic leg.

I insisted that he come inside before the thirty-kilometre trip home.

"I hit a porcupine on the way in here," Randy confessed over cranberry juice, "but them buggers is a dime a dozen."

"Right," I nodded.

"You ever eat porcupine pie?"

Randy and I spent two hours discussing roadkill, a subject he knew well, as he used to drive a shuttle bus that stopped each Friday at the parole office and a hospital. Porcupine can be stringy apparently, but nice when stuffed with sauerkraut or chopped apple. Squirrel should be marinated, preferably in moonshine. By the time we were finished, it was so dark that I had no choice but to offer him my couch to sleep on.

Given my situation, I probably spent too much time with Randy. By selling the concertina, I was trying to remove the clutter from my life, for I am, in the process, you see, of cataloguing the men I've dated. I have been wondering if, as someone wise once said, *"Fate is often met taking the road you chose to avoid it."*

No. 1: Miguel was my boyfriend in university. His parents lived in Mexico, where his father was an architect who restored pillaged haciendas, his mother an artist who worked in gold. Bohemians, they lived in a monastic house of adobe and timber beams.

We met in a political science class where we debated Chile, the CIA, and the Allende overthrow by Pinochet with a fervour that now seems odd. Miguel had brown eyes that were always squinted, as though the sun were scorching instead of diluted by fog. He was engrossed in *One Hundred Years of Solitude*, the epic novel of magic realism by Gabriel Garcia Marquez. His apartment was decorated with an omnipotent sun and woven rugs of geometric designs. I was away from my parents for the first time, and when I grew homesick, Miguel gave me earrings made from vintage *milagros*—Spanish for miracles—like those left at altars or placed on statues of Jesus. They come in many shapes: birds, horses, arms, legs. Mine were houses, and they were *real* gold, unlike the tin offerings sold to tourists.

Miguel showed me a photo of his parents outside the chapel of a once-grand hacienda, which had stables and a school ravaged by peasant armies. Tall and fair, his parents resembled bleached cornstalks on the burnt Latin landscape.

"Are you adopted?" I asked Miguel, who was as bronze as a glazed pot.

"Oh, no," he scoffed in horror. "I acclimatized to living in the sun."

One night, while naked and drunk on tequila, he told me something about nuns and an orphanage and a secret arrangement with his parents, all as fantastic as a Marquez angel falling to earth in a rainstorm. He mentioned *charros* and foreign bloodlines. I often wondered if that involuntary admission, induced by the heart of the blue agave plant and never repeated, doomed us.

"Should I meet you at the airport?" I asked after summer break.

"No," Miguel replied. "I won't be coming back."

In the following months, as I worked and studied, I felt numb, as though I had witnessed a tragedy. I could not associate the mangled flesh with human lives. Instead of following a path illuminated by ghosts, Miguel became a stockbroker in Mexico City.

I live in a sixty-unit building with six floors and a tenant base of seniors and gay schoolteachers in their forties. Crummy place, but I like the location, near the harbour and the train tracks I find as comforting as a white noise machine. The main problem is the wall, so thin that I can hear coughing and the *whirrrrrrrrr* of an electric toothbrush.

The teachers, who leave for long spells in summer, are agreeable and keep to themselves. The seniors are nosy and cranky. Whenever I venture out, I can feel their eyes upon me, as unyielding as Gulag guards.

"Mindless meddlers," I mutter when I catch two watching Randy, who walks straight-backed as though he's been fitted with a metal rod and halo.

The only conversations I can clearly make out come from 208, occupied by Iris and Don Black. After years of having the floor, Don, a retired TV correspondent, has been reduced to a recalcitrant audience of one. Whenever Iris attempts to break into his monologues, she is stopped with the abominable "When you see my lips moving, that means I am talking."

Many times, I have heard how Don, dressed in Innu wear, risked his life driving a snowmobile over the Labrador Sea in pursuit of news. He waited, as he tells victims in the laundry room, five years for a big story to break in northern Newfoundland. One day, the caps fell off his two front teeth, rendering him a walking lisp. Neither the medical clinic nor the hardware store, tired, I am sure, of his odious "When you see my lips moving...," would provide adhesives. Then a plane crashed on the ice, and a native freelancer went live to air for two days straight, winning awards that could have been Don's.

No. 2: Jonah was a fisheries observer who went to sea on foreign vessels to patrol Canada's two-hundred-mile limit. On one trip, a

drunk Russian held Jonah hostage with an AK-47; on another, a psychotic storm hurled him from his bunk.

Sensitive about occupational hazards such as scabies and lice, Jonah developed a series of social tics to elevate himself to a higher social order. As soon as we entered a house, *any* house, Jonah would point to the art and announce, "That picture is hung too high." Any time we were served vegetables, he would proclaim, before the humble rutabaga even touched his lips, "These are overcooked." And if the wine was German or sweet, he would cringe.

One summer, Jonah went away and left his big Labrador, Cowboy, with me. He needed to recharge, he explained, after a season filled with rumblings over silver hake and prostitutes and Cuban cigars.

While I was walking Cowboy, he viciously and without warning attacked a teacup poodle named Petunia, leaving only blood, fur, and a small mangled sweater. I was so upset that I drove two days, unannounced, to see Jonah. He answered his door wearing a black kimono with fiery dragons. Oddly enough, Jonah, that stickler for etiquette, had wrapped the robe incorrectly, overlapping the left side with the right, which in Japan is done with corpses.

"Oh, come in," he said. Then lifting one flowing kimono sleeve, he gestured to a woman with a jug of Lonesome Charlie. "This is Svetlana."

About ten years ago, I caught a random glance of Jonah. It was Boxing Day and he was standing in Canadian Tire in the endless returns line near a drafty door. The draft seemed unnecessarily cruel to shoppers who had already received unsuitable gifts. Jonah had a weary, disappointed look on his face, like perhaps he, too, had made bad choices. He had a wooden toilet seat tucked under one arm.

❀   ❀   ❀

I hear a play-by-number organ coming from 208, then recriminations.

While Don was pursuing his career, Iris had followed, taking lowly positions in rotating cities. She had been an on-air performer before she was uprooted and remains, to this day, bitter about her last makeshift job with a federal government department. In that job, Iris concocted studies that fell into two categories: "the happier at home" and "the not happier at home." Under the former were issues involving hospitals, institutions, and palliative care facilities. *"A study shows that mothers of quadruplets, released from hospital four hours after giving birth, are happier at home!"* Alzheimer's patients, terminally ill seniors, and transplant recipients were all happier at home, according to Iris's never-questioned studies. The only people *not* happier at home were toddlers under the care of their mothers. Under a plan to force women onto tax rolls, Iris manufactured young misfits who stared longingly out windows at the daycare children who trudged by in rain or snow, tied together like sled dogs.

Iris is resentful of this job, which seems to represent to her the cost of being young and following impulses as random as lightning. She mentions the studies whenever Don waxes about Press Gallery dinners or colleagues who addressed each other as "Senator," in the jocular tone of the compulsive gambler who makes light of his obsession but dreams of nothing else.

Meanwhile, I have seen the building superintendent sneaking into Ms. Whynacht's apartment after she leaves for school with her acoustic guitar and Jim Croce songbook.

After Miguel and Jonah, I entered a series of brief relationships, the kind you stumble into to erase traces of the last. Obliterators.

❀　❀　❀

No. 3: Victor had been a chubby child. To lose weight, he had limited his food consumption to one improbable item: french fries. To adhere to this diet, he frequented Chuckie's Chip Wagon and filled his freezer with frozen fries. One night, we went to an Italian restaurant with another couple.

"Do you have fries?" Victor asked, as if inquiring about the calamari.

"Uh, no." The waitress, dressed in black, as lovely as the decor, was a dark-haired vision who kept the orders in her head next to arias. She smiled sublimely.

"Then I will just have a gin and tonic."

To his credit, Victor was able to maintain his composure while the table became strained and awkward as though there had been an argument over the bill.

Once, at my insistence, Victor tried to eat a banana, but he regurgitated the foreign fruit in an episode so embarrassing for both of us that it spelled the end.

It's curious how time has stripped these events of emotion: pain, turmoil, melodrama. Now, they are all like old songs in my head, the words clear but too familiar to evoke passion.

Steven (No. 4) and his roommate, Mac, once staged a party on the train from Halifax to Moncton, playing ABBA songs the whole time. I'd never seen a Murphy bed before—their popularity peaked in the 1930s—but they let me sleep on theirs one night. Steven, I discovered while tracing past paramours, now runs an elegant bed and breakfast in the Annapolis Valley. It has wrought-iron beds, lush florals, and towels the colour of whipped butter. He and Mac are married.

On the train tracks, I see a girl in a black dress and matching hat with cat ears. I watch the Goth cat follow the tracks and I wonder if she plays the flute. I hope she does not live in the shrouded world of blogs, communing with outcasts who have names like *dark_heart*, narcissists who wallow in misery and threaten to dismember their parents or the night boss at Subway.

At some point, we are all like stray cats who drift from house to house, adapting to the food, smells, and rhythms, waiting for the owner who will define you with a name: Patches, Smokey, Career Woman, which you willingly accept in return for love, however depthless.

I see a taxi stop outside my building and deposit an ancient woman, so faded that I can hear her cells dying. She plants each foot carefully to avoid a fall and then, to my surprise, boots a discarded coffee cup. I've been to buildings that house a more sociable breed of seniors, the ones who play bridge and square dance, who feed squirrels and ducks, but this is not that place. This is the home of the disappointed and the deserted, a place to store regrets and harbour grudges.

No. 5: I met Warren when I was twenty-five and living in a village with antique stores and a blacksmith's shop. I was teaching Grade Four; he was working as a diver for an oil company. I had never lived in the country before, that enigmatic chunk of Canadiana, and I was overwhelmed by the stark beauty and crushing solitude. My school, a flat brick building, had seventy students but none of the charm of the two-room schoolhouse it had replaced.

It was November and the village was in that strange lull before the

streets were dressed for Christmas but after the summer accents—
the sailboats, antique hunters, and long-haired teens—had gone. A
black cat climbed in and out of a shop window, bored. A house in the
process of moving sat up on blocks. Stripped of summer bustle, the
village had reverted to a sturdy town of fishing and commerce. It
seemed emotionless, storing energy for the next kinetic burst.

Warren approached me at a coffee shop owned by Marg, who
drove a van. Marg had done a booming business all summer, but on
this day, three old ladies in thick sweaters were the only other customers. Rugged, with crinkly blue eyes, Warren appeared before me.

"Would you like to taste my carrot cake?" he asked with a voice
that suggested more.

"Okay," I replied for no sound reason.

Warren was older than most of the men I had dated, a free
spirit who had embraced the counterculture of the sixties, but
also had practical skills like fixing trucks and building furniture.
He had a spooky, peaced-out aura that was at odds with some of
his pursuits. While most hippies floated through the air, plumes
of beads and hair and alternative values, Warren took substantial
steps and only seemed wispy around the edges. He told me that
I reminded him of his girlfriend from high school, a Swedish
doctor's daughter, who had moved to New York. "We're still good
friends, though," he said, with that peaced-out look.

Warren had used LSD in high school, he told me, with his
friends, a married couple who now ran a local pottery shop. Before opening the shop, they had taught art in prison. When I met
them, it was clear by their smirks that Warren was considered a
ladies' man. There had been one relationship, longer and more
complex than the rest, which everyone alluded to. The others
seemed fleeting.

Warren had a way of looking at you so directly that you gulped.
"If we are going to be friends," he said one night, undressing me
in the potters' bathroom, "you are going to have to trust me."

He wore rough Icelandic sweaters and a silver elephant-hair bracelet. According to African legend, the bracelet assures the owner good health and fortune. The two movable knots represent the earth and nature, the four strands the seasons. "My parents don't know what to make of me," he laughed. "My father is a judge."

Warren rented an iron-red house outside the village. The wooden house sat on three acres of woodland, framed by a mat of shrubs and wildflowers. Warren filled the house with uncomfortable handmade furniture and the smell of elaborate meals. I loved the symmetry of the house, which, to me, reflected the orderliness of the first owner, a lobster fisherman named Stanley. On the front were two low windows and a central door painted black. Above the door was a dormer with a window that overlooked granite boulders and occasional deer. Both sides of the house had four windows.

It was one of those houses that idealistic couples restored, adding goats and sheep and children named Martha and Jake. I wondered what type of children Warren would raise: sensitive souls, or demons who ate peanuts on your porch and left the shells, which were, if you *didn't* already know, biodegradable.

One night while Warren was outside collecting firewood, I opened his dresser drawers. On top of his T-shirts, I saw a stack of photos of Warren and an old girlfriend, who, from her posture and their matching Icelandic sweaters, appeared to be substantial, entrenched, and, to my surprise, the potter.

At the time, I shared an apartment with Gail, another teacher, a pale ectomorph with legs like drinking straws, the same circumference from the ankles to the thighs. Her feet stuck out like scuba flippers. Gail walked as though she had just climbed out of a lake, feet apart, stiff-kneed. She had met a Mountie, who picked her up on a Harley which he drove at high speed without a helmet. In his house, Gail reported, aghast, he had pit bulls and loaded guns. One night, the Mountie told Gail that they had Warren under surveillance. For what? I asked, shocked, but Gail didn't know, and I had no reason to believe the brute, because Gail had twice come home sobbing.

"Are you okay?" I asked.

Sniffling, Gail refused to lift her shameful eyes. Gail and I were not men-pleasers, those puzzling mixes of acquiescence and allure, those strange creatures who, for no apparent reason, draw the opposite sex, as inexplicably as people who can grow giant pumpkins. We were *not* those women.

I continued to see Warren at his perfect house until he shot me. Not on purpose. He was aiming for the Mountie, who, in a blur, stormed through the black door and pinned Warren to the ground. The bullet pierced my chest and shattered my spine. I have been in a wheelchair ever since.

On Tuesday, I placed an ad in *Bargain Buyer.*

FOR SALE: Walrus tusks. An eclectic accessory for any home. Call Nancy.

So far, I have received two calls. One from Bedford, the other from a pleasant-sounding man named Floyd from the rural town of Wahoo. I have given Floyd directions to my apartment and told him where to park to avoid surveillance.

Blossom

Oran Hatcher was a smudge of a man, a slight, balding presence who slipped in and out of focus. He wore black glasses and his shoulders were rounded as though he had just been released from a straitjacket. Oran could have been twenty-five or forty.

He worked at the coffee shop I frequented, and he had a little shtick he never seemed to tire of. After Oran dropped a biscuit in a takeout bag, he spun the bag, sealing it with a neat, swift move he had perfected. "That will be eighty-five dollars," he would say through his nose, and if he received a loonie as payment, he would announce, "Here's your fifteen dollars change." Everyone played along.

Oran had one odd source of conceit: he was abnormally proud of his head size. Whenever he met people, he informed them that he was exempt from Nova Scotia's bike helmet law, which made allowances for religious headwear and craniums over sixty-four centimetres in circumference. "My head is sixty-five point two."

Oran had never owned a bicycle in his life, but he bought one so that he could ride without a helmet and explain to anyone he encountered that his head surpassed the regulation size. And then one night, while riding home from work, Oran was hit by a truck and killed, a tragedy that seemed both gratuitous and cruel.

Everyone in life wants to be known for *something*, and for Oran, it was his big head. As a child, I had been known as "the clumsy one," and I went to great lengths, in later years, to maintain that distinction, tripping over rugs and rolling down stairs until it all became too obvious. My sister was "the blinker," and she was forced to continue blinking well into her thirties. My grandmother, Nina, was the lively one who never showed her age.

And so it came as no surprise that Nina felt compelled to show her youthful vigour when I was married in St. Bartholomew's Church on the same day that Oran was killed.

"Oh, look at Nina dance," people noted when the music started.

On the dance floor, distorted by a strobe light, Nina hurled her body about in a herky-jerky motion. It was that old person dance that defied definition: a spastic combination of the Funky Chicken and The Twist. As the evening passed, and the guests' attention drifted to the bar and talk of a hockey game, Nina's motions became more desperate.

"Maybe you should have a rest," someone urged.

"Oh no," she protested. "I am not tired at all."

Nina was wearing a bright green dress (she was also known for being fond of the colour green), and when she collapsed to the floor, lights flashing around her, she did, for a moment, blend in with the indoor-outdoor carpeting. Nina was down for a full ninety seconds before someone noticed.

"Call an ambulance!" that person shouted. "Call 911. I think she's dead."

Nina and Oran were laid out in adjacent rooms at the Harbour View Funeral Home. People shuffled in, paid their respects, and shuffled out. The brutality of life is indiscriminate, I decided. It shows no mercy to the innocent or weak.

We lived in a small town, so the visitors knew both of the deceased and visited one room and then the other. Someone noted that Oran did not have a mean bone in his body; someone mentioned, as proof of his kind-heartedness, the fact that Oran doted on a family cat named Blossom, which his parents kept inside. If another cat came to their window, Oran—no matter what he had been doing—scrambled for Blossom and raised her to the glass. "Look look, Blossom. It's your friend. She likes you."

The day that Oran was killed, he was not carrying identification, but the ambulance attendant recognized him from the coffee shop and called his mother, who sobbed until her heart shattered into one million pieces. "He loved that cat, he truly did," said Oran's mother, who ensured that a picture of Blossom was displayed with all of the others.

In Nina's viewing room, our family had mounted, along with the conventional family photographs, a picture of Nina trying out Rollerblades when she was seventy, arms raised like a bank teller's during a stickup. Nina's energy had not been wasted on frivolous pursuits, someone made a point of saying; she was the first to help others in need. Did you know that when Oran was killed, he was wearing wool mittens that Nina had knit last winter? Nina had made thirty pairs in every imaginable colour combination, and then donated them to schoolchildren and people like Oran.

"Imagine that."

A short man in a trench coat moseyed into Nina's viewing room.

Billy Balcolm lived on Main Street in a room that had once been part of a jewellery store that specialized in birthstones and decorative plates. Billy's room did not have curtains, and when you walked down the sidewalk, you could see him, through the storefront window, folding laundry or rearranging the pieces on his chess board.

Billy removed a brown fedora and shook my hand. Decades

ago—during a trip to California—someone had mistaken him for Humphrey Bogart, or so the story went. Billy nervously checked his pockets for a smoke. And then, as though it was expected, he offered up a Bogie line, a sardonic quip that suggested life was best viewed through a blurred lens, an inebriated focus that softened the hard, mean lines around people like Nina and Oran, good souls who never, no matter how hard they tried, appeared on the scorecard of life.

"The problem with the world is that everyone is a few drinks behind," said Billy, who just then nodded at my broken foot. I shifted my weight on my crutches, and smiled.

Bittersweet Bratislava

Harry sweats when he eats. When June first noticed the moisture on her husband's forehead, Harry scoffed: "It's the spicy food." He tapped an innocent enchilada. "It's making me hot." When June later observed that Harry sweat while eating a banana, he scoffed again, "It's nothing," blotting his forehead dry. "It's nothing."

Before long, June had determined—with needless veracity—that Harry perspired while consuming chocolate pudding and ice cream sundaes. Takeout pizza and rice.

"It's sweat!" he blustered, inwardly horrified. "Have you never seen sweat?"

Mindful of his mysterious affliction, Harry looked up from his sandwich and instinctively, reflexively, wiped his brow. It was probably unnecessary. The woman staring down at him, a tourist, would not have noticed if his face had been dripping, if torrents of sweat had been racing down his cheeks in a human flash flood.

"Is that you?" She lifted a book from the table, and pointed to the author's photo.

"Yes." He noticed her lapel pin: a pink cowboy hat.

"It doesn't look like you." She stared accusingly. "You're a lot older in real life."

In real life. Harry was tempted to become philosophical, to rattle off a Dostoyevsky quote from *The Idiot*, the one about characters who are "more real than real life itself," but that would, he decided, have been pretentious. Instead, he rearranged his books, securing them as though a chance wind could blow through and scatter them like napkins at a picnic.

Harry had been at the table in the mall since 10 a.m. He had managed to sell—and autograph—one copy of his first book of poems. It was $15.99 and beautifully bound in an indigo card cover that added depth.

Harry finished his ham sandwich and wiped his brow. The sweat—great rolling globs—appeared regardless of the temperature or his activity level. Harry would sweat in frigid air-conditioned vaults; he would sweat if he was nibbling on a cucumber sandwich, absently and half-asleep, or ripping into a side of ribs like a hyena.

Harry noticed two men his age outside the drugstore. Leo Mousley, a retired English professor, was wearing a green Barbour coat and gum rubbers.

"How is Ruth?" Harry heard Leo inquire.

The other man—his name was Arnold—smiled too strenuously. Harry could not remember the last time he had seen Ruth, the wife, who had let her hair go white.

"She has a new dog, a poodle." Arnold's voice cracked. "It's keeping her busy."

"White?" asked Leo.

"Ahhhhhhhhhh, yes."

Leo nodded with the same sincerity that Harry had once seen on the faces of strangers who had not known how to react to his cancer, strangers who were surprised, sympathetic, but mainly, overridingly, thankful it was not them.

The men left; Harry gathered up his books and walked to the drugstore. It had been months since he'd seen Leo and Arnold, he realized, nearing the counter, and they both seemed as vague as memories. Leo had ignored Harry and his book. Leo considered

anything written after 1949 as "contemporary middlebrow fiction," a mindset that may have explained his failure to secure a
publisher for his own weighty novels. Leo had, for years, taken
out his frustration on first-year English students, failing one-third
of the class for nebulous problems with "structure" or coordinat-
ing conjunctions. Harry did not care about the snub.

He picked up a copy of a national newspaper and shuffled to
the cash. When Harry and June moved to Moose River, eschew-
ing suburbia, they were young enough to make the daily commute
to the city, where they purchased an array of reading material:
newspapers, magazines, and obscure journals. Moose River was
then an unpretentious town, a stripped-down town of old homes,
unassuming locals, and city folk like them who planted herb gardens and read newspapers from New York.

Harry sat on a bench with his paper. Harry's publisher had told
him, with palpable excitement, that the newspaper was review-
ing his book of poems. After thirty years in the news business,
Harry had vowed not to get worked up over reviews. He did, after
all, remember the time that his own newspaper had sent Clary
Taylor to review a production of *Guys and Dolls*, and Clary, whose
idea of culture was strippers at the Captain's Cabin, found the
play "most unsatisfying."

Harry flipped the paper and, yes, there it was: his photo, the
same one that appeared on his book cover, taken two years after
June's death and one year after his bout with cancer. A headline.
And a full column review which Harry skimmed until he hit the
critical part. *"Harry Lawlor is a lousy poet who chooses even lousier
subjects."* And then, three paragraphs later: *"Maybe we should all
care about the author's ravaged prostate and his deceased wife.
Maybe not."*

❀   ❀   ❀

Harry shuffled into his bedroom and shoved the review under the bed where he could no longer see it. Maybe the book was weak—he had no idea if it *was* any good—but why, Harry wondered, had the reviewer made it so bloody personal?

Harry decided to go for a walk, following the route that he and June had habitually taken. In the distance, he saw a local character approaching on a bicycle. The man was wearing a grey beard and a white hockey helmet with the chin strap unbuckled. Completing the outfit were brief shorts from the John McEnroe era and a threadbare T-shirt with stripes. The shorts—once rudely referred to as grape smugglers—barely covered his privates. Behind him, the man was hauling a covered wagon that swung from side to side as though it were being whipped. For a moment, Harry wondered if there was a child inside, and then spotted two bags of groceries. For some reason, Harry felt cheated.

The bike passed, and Harry saw Richard Vachinski, a retired cellist, approaching on foot with a tiny white dog on a leash. Sheepish, Richard lowered his eyes, avoiding contact as a tour bus stopped behind him. Harry, on the other hand, brightened.

In Harry's town of Moose River, a town of self-doubt and changed expectations, the tiny white dogs were a signal, like smoke rising from the Vatican or empty vodka bottles in the trash. The white dogs belonged to a smattering of breeds: poodles, bichon frises, Shih Tzus, Maltese, and West Highland white terriers, many prone, it was discovered far too late, to a baffling ailment that caused shaking and tremors. In struggling houses, coping houses, the trembling dog was a panacea. It became the focus, the means for ignoring all immediate failings and disappointments. "White shaker syndrome," owners reported, relieved, it seemed, to have something remarkable to grasp.

Harry and June had made a game out of counting the dogs, always white, and usually woolly, the universal sign, they decided, for distress.

❀   ❀   ❀

The publisher, the same one who had sent the newspaper his book, shot Harry a disappointed email: *Too bad about the review!* Harry shrugged. What was *he* supposed to do? A few hours later, his daughter, Carmen, emailed him the blistering review in its entirety.

Disappointment dripped from the computer screen like tears. It was their fault that Carmen was so frail, Harry admitted to himself, because he and June had shielded her from the harshness of life. Carmen had the convex forehead and wide-set eyes of a picky eater. When she was young, Harry had driven her to a private school in Halifax, to an enclave of Volvos and *Save the CBC* signs erected by scholarly parents, who made low guttural noises they may or may not have been aware of.

Harry replied, trying to sound unruffled: *Thanks dear. Hope all is well.*

An hour later, another email from Carmen, who had Googled the reviewer and sent his photo as an attachment. *HERE HE IS!!!* And then to Harry's surprise: *THE BASTARD.*

Harry opened the attached file and a saw a dour, bald man, who appeared forty-five. In the photo, the critic was wearing leather chaps and posing with his own book. Was this a test? Harry wondered, as though he had not been tested enough. The chaps were obviously a statement. Of what? Harry had never identified himself by an ideology or a political bent, and he was hardly judgmental. He knew people from all walks of life, people of every colour, religion, and lifestyle; he'd worked with alcoholics, coke addicts, two Croatians, an American draft dodger, an insufferable South African, and a married man who underwent a sex change and then became a witch. He'd liked them all except for the South African, who had a habit of overtalking.

❀   ❀   ❀

Before June was diagnosed, in that uneasy time when they sensed that something was wrong, they bickered. Their argument, which lasted on and off for weeks, was over something that did not matter, something easy and meaningless to attack. It had started on a Sunday morning when Harry was in his den studying a website, his brow furrowed. The weekend before, he had travelled to Ottawa for a reunion of former newspaper columnists, a trip that had left him invigorated.

"What are you looking at?" June asked.

"We're thinking of nominating Randy Lungstrum for an Order of Canada."

"*Order of Canada?*" The words escaped in one incredulous laugh.

"He deserves it." Harry bristled. "The man is the dean of Canadian columnists."

June stared at Harry, giving him time to reconsider.

For years, Randy Lungstrum had written *Happenings on Top of the Hill,* an inane Ottawa column that chronicled singalongs, debates, and the much-anticipated Sexiest MP Contest. A perennial hit at the Press Gallery Dinners, Lungstrum did impersonations of Joe Clark *and* Maureen McTeer. Lungstrum had a thin, strangulated voice that escaped in the sharp bursts of a smoke detector, and yet he never missed a chance to perform. Upon retiring, he penned a two-hundred-page autobiography that exposed the depth of his madness. "Could I have made a career of singing?" he asked rhetorically. "I really don't know."

"The man is an idiot," said Joan.

"You don't understand. You've never worked in Ottawa."

"I understand that he got caught exposing himself in a hot tub," she countered.

"That's not the point. He is still The Dean."

❀   ❀   ❀

Another letdown email from the publisher. Two stores were re-turning books, Harry was informed. He put on his coat and drove, as furtively as he had mailed in Lungstrum's nomination, to the nearest bookstore, a modest operation run by a man with a silver ponytail.

In the back of the store, Harry found the reviewer's own novel and turned it over. There was the photo in the leather chaps, and another shot of the author in a purple fedora with an eagle feather. Harry skimmed the first chapter; he read the back jacket and the final four pages. *Bittersweet Bratislava* was a lustful international romance filled with "suspense and burning hot sex scenes." Harry reshelved the book and shuffled to the street.

Back home, Harry patted his forehead dry as he finished supper. After June had drawn it to his attention, he'd researched the sweating. He believed it was connected to a childhood injury; some moron had once sliced his cheek with a golf club. Harry had convinced himself that it was gustatory sweating or Frey's Syndrome, caused by an injury of the auriculotemporal nerve. June, who seemed to take the whole thing as a joke, suggested it could be fatal.

The sweating did start, Harry acknowledged, around the same time that Moose River, their smug comeback to suburbia, was transformed from an understated village into the home of the Bonnie Breeze Museum. Delivered before a provincial election, the two-million-dollar museum was built on Main Street, a flat prefabricated building topped by a gigantic pink cowboy hat. The hat—the Grand Ole Opry singer's trademark—contained speak-ers that blasted Bonnie's greatest hits, including "Night Falls Like a Guillotine" and the maudlin "Little Smiling Babies." Open from May until December, the museum offered special rates for sen-iors, bus tours, and members of Bonnie's International Fan Club.

By the time the project was announced, there was no time for protest, particularly from people who were not, in the true sense of the word, locals. Nobody cared that Bonnie Breeze had actually been born *outside* Moose River; nobody cared that "Little Smiling Babies" was unbearably mawkish.

The museum didn't faze June, who had a highly developed sense of the absurd. After a day of tour buses and testimonials, June would insist that they do something odd like attend a cat show at the mall, where they would sit in the front row, spellbound. She would gasp when the winner was announced, and note: "You can never go wrong with a coon cat." June would locate the owner of the homeliest cat—a ratty tortoiseshell with one bad eye—and say, with enough conviction that even Harry believed her, that she had never seen such remarkable markings. The owner, a young boy, would beam.

Harry, on the other hand, felt changed, undeniably diminished by the hoopla. The BB hand towels, the fans who knocked on doors seeking Breeze relations, the fanatics who wore pink cowboy hats and followed the singer on tour, calling themselves The Bonnie Five. The credit cards stamped with a photo of Bonnie's face, musical notes escaping from her mouth as cleverly as she had escaped her stifling beginnings.

After the museum opened, Harry acted abnormally for a while. To establish his worldliness, he had started to use the word *bodega* in conversations. He had never even heard the word, he later admitted, until he started watching cop shows on TV. Suddenly, every time he turned on the TV, someone was being gunned down in a bodega manned by a frantic Vietnamese man last seen reaching for the under-the-counter buzzer. Ice-T was often involved.

And then one day, after an animated phone call, Harry stood before June in the den.

"Did you see the news?" he demanded. He was wearing the look of someone who had, in a manic moment, purchased a car without admitting he was broke.

"No," June confessed.

"Randy Lungstrum has been named to the Senate."

"That's terrible."

"Why?" Harry demanded. "Why is that terrible?"

"Because he is an alcoholic and a sycophant."

"Well." Harry fumbled for a response, through the panic that had clouded his thinking. "They have to come from somewhere."

June frowned again, and Harry stared at her defiantly, but his eyes were too wide and too unseeing. Was it age? The sweating? Or the same befuddlement that caused him to close the electronic car windows without checking to see if June had a hand extended? Or was it something else, the knowledge that his life was about to be shattered?

Harry had once worked with a night editor named Dougal, a surly chap who answered the phone with a lung-clearing sigh. At the age of forty-seven, Dougal had received a terminal diagnosis. Co-workers who previously could never find anything good to say about Dougal gushed about how brave he was, how courageously he was facing death. Days before Dougal died, Harry visited him in the hospital.

"I wish I was scared, Harry," the desker said without flinching. "I wish I was angry. The sad part is I just don't give a fuck."

Harry wanted to give a fuck. He wanted to feel indignant about his merciless review; he wanted to see the humour and humanity in the hapless Bonnie Five. He wanted something, anything, to override this vacuum in his soul that June had left, that insensate state of being, humbled to the point where he moved through time, naked and numb, impervious to everything around him, a firewalker treading over life's emotions, scorched and dead.

❀　❀ ・❀

In the distance, Harry saw the bearded man on the bicycle. Instead of the grape smugglers, he was wearing a baggy Speedo, an indecent, chlorine-ravaged rag. Behind him, the covered wagon weaved like a drunk who could, at any moment, stumble into traffic.

Harry nodded at Deverell Flewelling, a PhD in astrophysics, who had battled irrelevance by becoming aggressively eccentric and thrusting his nearly naked body parts in people's faces. A one-man assault on the senses, Deverell played the bagpipes, he cooked smoked eel, and he puffed on a pipe as though his superior intelligence gave him licence to offend.

Harry thought about Arnold and Leo; he thought about thwarted dreams and youthful expectations. After the novelty had expired, living in Moose River was, for the urban expats, like living in a garden maze: confined, benumbed, stripped of stimulation. You walked round and round the town until one day your panic turned to resignation and your skin smelled like ennui, and when all else had failed, when no one cared and no one rallied, and the apocalyptic bottom was heading toward you like the bumper of a tour bus, the tiny white dog appeared.... It was all okay when June was here.

Coming over a hill was Arnold's wife, Ruth, moving at a crisp pace, a disc player strapped to her waist. Her hair, once white and as lifeless as insulation, was now mahogany. She pulled off her headphones.

"Bichon frise?" she asked Harry, panting.

"Yes, she is," said Harry, nodding at the animal. "Ten months old."

"Lovely." Ruth waved goodbye.

The tiny white dog trembled, then trotted off, and Harry, arm extended as though he had purpose, bravely, stoically, followed.

Hank Williams Is Coming to Save Us

It looked like a pretty good gig: Agatha Willows, managing editor. There wasn't much to manage: two reporters and a kraut-eating town of five thousand souls, but then again I wasn't much of an editor.

"I have some projects in mind," I lied. To myself, to my ever-hopeful mother, like I wasn't thirty-five and fried.

"Writing?"

"Uh, yeah. Writing projects and stuff."

For three hundred and fifty dollars a month, I rented half of a rose-coloured house with dormers. My bedroom had a hardwood floor and a view of the harbour. From my window, I could watch the fleet of pickups at the government wharf; I could see lobster boats moored three deep with orange rain gear hung on hooks. In the wee hours, I could see Jim's Taxi (*Call Anytime*) dropping off deckhands with duffel bags.

The ocean, a source of sustenance and danger, gave the town a heightened air. It was as though you never knew who could sail into port on a wooden schooner; someone exotic with a tan and an accent and a knife strapped to his belt. It was a town with long lulls punctuated by big catches and fast farewells. People worked hard, on boats and in shipyards, and they moved with the poise of men who could make things with their hands and women who could withstand loss.

I bought a Tancook schooner, a thirty-four-foot proletarian that transcended class. Built as a swordfishing vessel, *Parmilla G.* was everything I wasn't by then: hard-working, stable, and sound. Black with a buff deck, she offered me solitude, freedom, and one last chance for salvation.

I was downtown buying deck paint when the Reardons drifted through the fog in a green Citroën. I remember that fog: dry ice rising from the feet of a rock pretender, schlocky Vegas fog. At the time, I didn't know what social current brought them to Nova Scotia. Some said it was "the draft"; some said there had been a family tragedy too painful to discuss.

"I'm Tom Reardon from Lexington." He shook my hand, sending shocks of testosterone up my arm. "I hear this is good country for sheep."

"Sheep?"

He wasn't listening for my response, just measuring his impact on the world. I enjoyed talking to Tom, I decided then and there at the checkout. I could think bad thoughts and he would never notice.

"I'm planning to take a shepherd's workshop in Stowe," Tom announced. "To earn my spurs docking tails with a hot iron or blade." Grinning, with spittle at the corners of his beard, he looked like a Hollywood Viking: big, barbarous, stomping about in blood-caked boots. Someone said that Tom had been a Green Beret, but then again Americans were always overwritten. This was the seventies, remember, with free love, Vietnam, and *Dirty Harry.*

Tom and his wife had three teenagers: two boys and a girl named Ceecee. Tom's wife, Viv, was plain and preternaturally chirpy, using exuberance to close the genetic gap between them. "My mutth-ahh belonged to the same historical society as Eleanor Roosevelt," I heard her boast over fabric bolts in Healey's Dry Goods, which sold everything from work shirts to Mercury outboard motors. In Levi's and cropped hair, Viv was as sexless as an atrophied jockey. Her nose was long, the tip curiously flattened as though it were pressed against glass.

Before long, word spread across the wharves and through the streets about the new people: the Americans. There was talk of French antiques, Hahhh-vahhhd, a New York family business as the rumours floated like sea smoke.

"Them folks like to tell their business," noted Mildred Healey, who owned the dry goods store.

"As long as they don't go fencing off the blueberry bushes like those last people," warned her husband, Ira, who hadn't eaten a blueberry in thirty years.

Tom bought an ocean lot at a tax sale and then moved an empty Cape Cod to the site. In some small towns, taking a person's property in a tax sale is like lifting the watch off a corpse, but the Reardons didn't seem to care. The move was dramatic. I ran a shot of the house: one hundred years old and mortified to be crossing Back Bay on oil drums.

For the move, Tom hired Nathan Smith, a retired skipper. Nathan usually sat on his back step carving ducks. He accepted life's twists and, after decades of chasing fish and battling gales, trusted each man to do his best. Nathan had two brothers listed on a granite memorial downtown. Hastings and Moyle had been deckhands on the *Matilda May*, which was lost off Sable Island in 1950 in a storm that old men claim broke from the bottom of the sea in a Biblical explosion of fury.

"Nathan is the best mover in the county!" declared one of Tom's boys, who called everyone, even corroded skippers, by their first names.

I christened the boys Ragnar Short Legs and Leif Chicken Neck. Next to Tom, the teens seemed puny. All day long, they fired up make-and-break engines, and it seemed a mockery, really, of the boys who'd died too young and the widows who'd stood in wait.

Occasionally, I would see Ragnar and Leif at the government wharf rescuing cast-off boats which they would eventually discard. I could smell their hollowness; it was the same rank scent that followed me to sea. Sometimes, I sailed to an island inhabited by fishermen and wild rose bushes. It had houses that smelled like seaweed and sand.

The newspaper was small-time, but I needed a second chance after my flame-out in Toronto. Sober, I would never have sent those letters; I never would have become a tired cliché: office romance with a married man. Chuck was an alcoholic sportswriter who lurched from one affair to the next, sobering up long enough to divorce his wife and marry a twenty-year-old waitress from a strip club.

There were enough routine stories in town to keep me busy. Once in a while, an offshore crew would let off steam. Tough men with limps and leather jackets. Some had Newfoundland accents. Good hearts dogged by bad luck. It never amounted to much; any real trouble was down the highway, outside town in a dogpatch of trailers and shacks.

Occasionally, I got a call from a national magazine seeking notes for major stories of interest elsewhere. When Skylab was crashing and there were rumours it was headed to Nova Scotia, I was paid eighty dollars to drive down the coast before it came down off Australia.

Like most fishing towns, this one was steeped in superstition: Never say *pig* on a ship; never wear grey mittens on board. For luck, give your boat a name with three As, such as *Mafalda* or *Lavinia May*. The town harboured a fear of outsiders who could—through their mere presence—upset the balance of life. People liked to tell a cautionary story about a luckless town that had lost its fish. When that town was young, the church had built a convent. It sent six nuns, including Sister Theresa, a sprightly girl with a bicycle. Over the years, as the fishery started to fade like cotton curtains in the sun, the convent grew smaller and smaller until only Sister Theresa remained, an apparition in a black habit and plastic shoes.

One day, the sun was bright, as though someone had removed the natural filter of dampness and fog. Sister Theresa saw a man hobbling down the road in tight jeans and cowboy boots. He had a leather jacket slung over one shoulder, hooked on a finger, and he was shirtless. His skin was blindingly white, the kind of skin that had never seen a beach or a Mediterranean sun.

Theresa nodded at the man. And then she walked to the gas station slowly, as if she were under a spell, and hammered a Ford LTD with a mallet over and over again. Then a pickup truck. "Destroy your TVs!" she shouted, "and radios!" She'd been ordered to turn back time, she announced, to avoid the looming Judgment Day. "Hank Williams is coming to save us on a big white steed!"

Not long after, the fish disappeared. "See," people said, as though something had been proven. "See what happens."

Viv planted a kaleidoscope of wildflowers and installed a wooden front door she had salvaged from an abandoned house. Tom converted the fish shack into a painting studio for Viv, who dabbled in watercolours. Their house, which she had named Christian's after its original owner, was *her* doing, her design. It had white walls trimmed with scrimshaw. Oak floors and sextants. I expected more from Tom: a turf-covered longhouse with an open pit for cooking. "Arrrrr," his thick chest heaving like ocean swells as he declared, "that was a good job of work." Tom was as phony as punched pollock, but I liked his bravado.

After a few months, an uncle visited. He was from Viv's side, they said. Pale and porcine, he had a skin disease that left white flakes in his wake. He talked with a lisp. For a piss-tank in a rusty Pinto, he was a hell of a snob. He had taught school somewhere, and he was always waxing about Groton and Reverend Endicott Peabody. He liked to bait Tom in public, taunting him with insults about the Republicans or guns: "Go ahead, thhooot me, you warmonger."

I saw him in the Below Deck Tavern glaring at a waitress. "When you are through communicating missives of thuuuch vital import," he sputtered, "I would like another beverage." When the family couldn't stand him anymore, when he'd pissed the spool bed yellow and turned Tom red with rage, they poured him into the exploding Pinto and sent him onto the highway, hoping he would die.

Everyone knew the Gordons were trash: not county hosers with Ski-Doos and babies named Sherrisse, but unabashed trash. "Crazy as Luke's dog," as the saying went, "and he died howling at the moon." The Gordons lived in a dogpatch in a double-wide trailer with dogs.

It was the youngest Gordon—Dirt, they called him—who Ceecee moved into Christian's that winter. Just seventeen, Dirt was the top scallop hand in Nova Scotia. Elden Howse, Captain Highliner for four years, had his pick of men, and he always took Dirt. Dark and unreachable, Dirt was handsome, one of those genetic mutations God creates as a joke. His mother looked like

Jackie Gleason, and the list of possible fathers was a *Who's Who* of bottom-feeders, but Dirt had the face of an angel and curly black hair.

Ceecee was as fair as Dirt was dark. Small like Viv, she had the same dented nose. She reminded me of a snake, with cleaved hair covering the corners of wide-set eyes. She had a spooky smile, and if you asked me the colour of her eyes, I'd say yellow even today, even though I know that couldn't be right.

One day at the post office, she cornered me.

"Agatha, you were in a dream of mine. Dirt and I were going to Europe and taking Mother's horse, Celeste."

She had a face that brought out the best and worst in men.

"Really?" I asked, wondering what she *really* meant. "Was I going too?"

"No, but you took our picture with a Leica and said, 'Have a nice trip.'" She smiled as if I'd done something cool. "So *I* said, 'If you see a man without a smile, give him one of yours.'" She walked away.

This was during the scallop boom on Georges Bank, and Dirt was raking in over sixty grand a year. Scallopers were blowing their shares on jukeboxes and jacked Mustang Cobras. Satellite dishes sprouted near customized vans with naked nymphs and Gothic dragons. Mildred Healey's son bought a Mustang Boss 429, but I didn't begrudge him because it was hard, mean work. I saw a scallop boat turn turtle from ice one February, and I was there when they brought in a deckhand torn up by a winch.

With his share, Dirt bought Ceecee a fox-fur coat. He gave the parents a dormant sail loft that added a thin veneer of purpose to their lives. It was all Dirt could do after Tom's sheep, which may have had a disease, ate themselves to death. By all accounts, it was ghastly: two hours of convulsions and frothing mouths as the gluttonous sheep collapsed, necks as stiff as ironing boards.

"Damn sheep," was all Tom said. Viv was always *on*, but on

those days Tom moved through life in a dark sulk, as though his good looks and Viking strength were all he needed to contribute.

Tom was at the sail loft the night that Dirt's largesse ended in a crash outside town. I heard the call on my scanner. Dirt was older and harder by then, with a goatee and rough tattoos. Volunteer firemen used pry bars to peel back the wheelhouse of his truck, which was folded as tight as an origami frog.

After the crash, Viv made more noise than a flock of gulls at a dumpster: *Dirt would be flown to the Mayo Clinic, a doctor from Boston would oversee his care...* Her munificence knew no bounds. By the time Dirt was sprung from a Halifax hospital ward, all his belongings had been dumped in Dog Patch, Ceecee had gone to live with the uncle in New Hampshire, and Dirt was adrift, a one-legged deckhand no one would touch.

It was a Friday night and Christian's was smothered by a cold grey fog. Not Vegas fog, schlocky and staged, but a rubber tarp of dampness. The perpetrator used a scalloping knife, said the police report, a blunt-edged device wielded with uncommon force. The male victim's arms showed defence wounds, while the female was attacked with extreme rage. I know he was big and dark as ten fathoms, but I still can't figure how he killed them both, not with Tom a Green Beret, not with him a cripple. "Messy as a bucket of fish guts," said a source. "Don't go printin' that."

I covered Dirt's trial, and his lawyer said he was a heroin addict, an abused child; that he really loved the snake-eyed girl. Dirt had a full beard by then which gave his face a Christlike look. One pantleg was pinned at the knee. Dirt couldn't read, his lawyer said; he was ADD or OCD or something in between. Ragnar and Chicken Neck took the stand but added nothing of substance, just sobs and whimpers; so on and on it went without any sense. Maybe Dirt was like Odin and turned into a beast.

They buried Viv, but the boys freed Tom, casting his ashes into the wind. Tom's remains landed in a sweet cove where the sun was bright and minke whales fed on mackerel. I think he was relieved.

Mildred Healey, who knew the owner of the funeral home, said the whole mess was built on a pile of lies that had collapsed like rotten staging. There was no New York business; Tom was broke and Viv was planning to sell antiques. According to Mildred, it was "all chowdered up. The uncle wasn't *really* the uncle; he was Viv's no-good first husband. The kids were *his*, you know, Tom just raised them."

I knew all this, but I couldn't tell, not after all I'd learned about keeping secrets.

Mildred said Dirt had phoned Ceecee in New Hampshire the day before *it* happened. The uncle took the phone and called Dirt an illiterate gimp and a retard. Mildred, who cleared Dirt's account of debt, said you couldn't trust outsiders, especially Americans who would fence off a blueberry patch that people had picked for years and then use Elgie Nowe's wharf without asking. Why Elgie's family had owned that wharf for eighty years!

The next day I drove to a beach with a boardwalk and an ice cream stand. With the tide out, seagulls left prints on the wet sand while plovers darted, traceless.

A bus arrived with four elderly ladies in wheelchairs. White-haired, two had woollen blankets covering their legs. They reminded me of hydrangeas in the last days of fall, colourless blossoms that were slowly but absolutely nearing the end. Once they were in place, a caretaker shuffled down the line. "Strawberry? Chocolate?" she asked, but the answers were inaudible. "Oh," she smiled at the frailest. "I'll surprise you."

Against a soundtrack of seabirds and guttural engines, the sea was moving so gently that I could almost forget how lethal it could be. I could almost forget the fatherless children and the headstones that promised *Earth has no sorrow that Heaven cannot heal.* And all the while, one of the ladies cradled a form in her arms, swathed in a baby blanket. She rocked it, leaning forward to kiss the top of its head. She pulled back the blanket, exposing the skull, and I saw that it was a doll. She kissed the doll, and I wondered how many babies she had cradled, how many hearts she had soothed in the cruel seas of life.

The magazine was paying me a hundred bucks to dig a little deeper. Find someone close to the Reardons, it said, put a face on the dead. A southerly breeze was blowing as I walked uptown, searching veiled windows and widow's walks for clues. I needed someone to eulogize Tom, to make him greater than this tawdry ending.

Viv thought the town was a movie set for a feature film starring William Hurt, but Tom knew it was real: a hard town with history, a town made anxious by outsiders, even elderly nuns. Deep down, I think, he understood. At least that's what I reasoned when we went for covert sails on *Parmilla G.*, free to be who we were: weak and flawed and selfish. Some think a small town is confining, but only for the people born there, the ones who count. For the people like me and Tom—the people who never belong and never really *want* to—it's all the same.

Doll and Snooks

Arabella was a war bride.

Like many drawn by love and dreams, by hardship and misfortune, she arrived in Canada through Pier 21. The trip over was arduous, with all of the wives and babies jammed in one area, seasick. A Scottish stewardess named Nell tended the flock. "Make yourselves look lovely now, ladies," she urged as the ship entered Halifax Harbour. "Brighten up!"

Just as the ship passed Georges Island, a ferrous fog lifted, and it was as though someone had taken a cloth and wiped the steam from a bathroom mirror. Everything was suddenly clear: the crowds, the bands, the sailboats. Arabella stepped off that wharf and straight into the arms of Snooks, whom she had never met before. Her husband, an air force corporal named Pepin, was late, and by the time he had raced from a cab and onto that pier, Arabella had fallen under the spell of Snooks and his dashing, hypnotic demeanour. Snooks liked to wear cocky hats and grey flannel suits. He called her Doll.

Over forty thousand war brides landed at Pier 21, and to commemorate that social phenomenon, a plaque was erected. Many of the brides boarded trains that took them to lives they could barely imagine, with kinfolk who had strange accents and queer tastes in food. Outhouses, woodstoves, and miles of black spruce as endless as the sea.

"No need to worry," Snooks promised Doll. "I'm a city boy."

While Pepin's family operated a farm in northern New Brunswick, Snooks's mother was a North End bootlegger, an entrepreneur in a neighbourhood of stevedores and glass-eyed survivors of the 1917 blast that had shattered the city. In that milieu, near a dump and a prison, Winnie sold shots at twenty-five cents apiece to abattoir workers. To avoid getting busted, Winnie had a couple of hides; one was under a bedroom floorboard, the other beneath shingles on the back of the house.

"One night, when someone pimped to the cops, she threw a quart from a window," explained Snooks, who liked to embroider his tales. "She hit a prison guard on the head."

"No damage done, I hope." Doll widened her eyes.

Within a few years, Snooks and Doll moved to a neighbourhood of wooden bungalows with trim yards and radios that played, instead of war songs, "Zip-a-Dee-Doo-Dah."

Doll had black hair brushed back to her shoulders, a casual but glamorous style, with a part to the left. While many ladies spent their nights in steel curlers to achieve the effect, Doll was blessed with a natural wave. Doll had a few odd habits. She kept all of her photos locked in a trunk and she obsessively checked for mail. It was though she was expecting something life-altering, such as a letter telling her she had won the Irish Sweepstakes, which had been on everyone's mind since the newspaper ran a story about a man who had won, and then squandered his prize. "What an idiot," people scoffed. "To get a chance like that..." To which Doll would shrug: "It's not the end of the world."

It was the same view she took when anyone raised her brief marriage to Pepin, the Air Force man. "He got over it," she said. "We had known each other for three weeks, and it was war with everyone racing off in all directions." When people suggested there had to be more, Doll added: "He was *French.* I hardly understood a word he said."

"Uh huh?"

"And he was always late."

Snooks never mentioned Pepin any more than he would expect Doll to bring up that little waitress from Derry. That was wartime, with its own code and rules. If you were in the war with someone, you never squealed if he was weak or sick, if he hid below deck and sobbed while U-boats circled, because you were in it *together* and the code applied. "I got two things out of the war," Snooks would joke to strangers, "a metal plate in my head and all the words to 'The Siegfried Line.'"

Snooks liked to hum a few bars on his way home from his job at the dockyard. At night, as a sideline, he trained fighters who picked him up in big cars and trucks. Before long, Doll met a wizened promoter named Jackie and a stupendous Jamaican who heard voices. The heavyweights dwarfed Snooks, while the feathers were as tight as jockeys. Some had jobs as barbers or mechanics; others did nothing but fight, like their fathers and brothers before them. They came from Montreal, New Glasgow, and Moncton. Snooks told funny stories about fighters who threw up in the rings or forgot how to count; he kept it as light as footwork.

Snooks had a heavy bag in the garage and smelling salts in the medicine cabinet. Downstairs, he stored boxing boots, gloves, a speedball, skipping ropes, and a red satin robe. The den was stacked with *Ring Record Books,* which made for absorbing reading, and before long, Doll could recite the weight classes like other people could name the planets: flyweight (112 pounds) through to heavyweight (over 175). In the margins, in barely legible writing, Snooks made notations on unknown opponents from New York or Cleveland. Some used fake names, he explained; some shaved their age. The book carried the measurements of all heavyweight champs, which, at one point, placed Jess Willard as the tallest at six foot six and a quarter, and gave Primo Carnera the largest neck at twenty inches.

Snooks had been in the book at one time, along with two of his brothers. The younger one, Spud, acted like a tough guy, and children could never tell if it was a put-on or not. A bouncer, he had the crushed nose and puffy eyes of a pug. Timmy had a friendlier disposition but was ironically more resilient in the ring. He was a charmer with big pipes and a shock of curly blond hair that reminded Doll of sunshine.

Across the street from Doll and Snooks lived the Sullivans. Stanley was a mailman who drank too much. Olive, the mother, raised the four children the best she could on instant milk, canned meat, and the odd treat of tapioca pudding. Olive acted as though she had something to be ashamed of, and the children had the same unworthy look, like orphans left for the state to raise.

One day, a teacher asked the Grade Fours to itemize their most recent dinner, and when she started with Peter Sullivan, who had cardboard in his shoes, he said, "Pork."

"Pork and what?" the teacher demanded. This was a few years after bureaucrats, spurred by wartime food shortages and malnutrition, released the *Canada Food Guide*, that often-irrelevant pyramid of grains, fruits, vegetables, protein, and fats.

"Pork and potatoes."

"What other vegetables did you have?"

"Mmmm?" Face flushing.

"What fruit?"

"Mmmm?"

When Peter finally said he couldn't remember, she stood him a corner where he peed his woollen pants. Peter was a plain boy with lifeless hair and an overbite, the kind of kid who played for hours on the railway tracks, a trace of bone and skin and modest expectations you feared would someday vanish.

Doll heard about the incident from her son and waited the following day for the teacher outside the school. Doll wore a belted green dress that matched her eyes. When you'd seen wards of maimed amputees, when you'd crouched in bomb shelters, sucking air through a rubber gas mask, you weren't afraid of a saucy teacher from Cape Breton.

"I'm wondering, Miss MacIsaac, what town are you from?"

"Why, Sydney Mines."

"And do they teach manners there?"

"I don't know what you mean."

"Where I come from, we learn manners at an early age, and we learn that they are extended to people of all ages. I'm not talking about which fork to use or how to fold a napkin, I'm talking about human kindness."

It was the only time anyone remembered Doll making a fuss over anything. Because Doll was the only English lady most knew, they assumed that she was the model: polite but coolly distant. Harry Jones, who lived two streets over, was a Brit, but he was a *man,* and he wore his birthplace like a merit badge, riding a Raleigh folding bicycle and harassing the newspaper for English soccer scores. Doll was private.

Life went back to normal after that. This was a time when television had two channels, when boys carried plastic guns and baseball mitts. Kids played War. Families of six drove VW bugs with babies stuffed in the back. People could air their differences and then move on.

And that's the way it was until Billy Windsor died in the ring and Snooks had to go see Billy's mother, who cried like she was carrying more pain than a human could bear. Billy had a brush cut and pale skin that turned blotchy when hit. It hadn't been a war like the battle that, years later, killed Duk-Koo Kim; it was an undercard with a few good flurries and a knockdown in the fourth. Why? people wondered. Why?

Doll never went to another fight and never allowed another word about the game inside her house. It was as though one more death was too much to bear. After that, Snooks waited outside for his drivers and the fighters were faceless *Ring* entries without families. That was how Doll dealt with pain: she slammed the door and bolted it tight.

By the time the letter arrived, the one Doll had been expecting, Stanley Sullivan had retired and stopped drinking. Doll saw the new postman, a young chap in shorts, put the letter in her box. Rushing out, she grabbed it and stuffed it in a drawer, return address hidden. Doll held her breath like she was back in a shelter, waiting for raiders to pass, merciless attackers who boasted about their kills on German radio before the bodies had been counted. Minutes later, she removed the letter, folded it like a dinner invitation, and left it on the bed for Snooks to read.

Doll sat in her chair. Closing her eyes, she saw herself in an English town with Georgian windows, driving down a road shaded by a canopy of branches. She saw herself stopping at a low house with a hopeful red door, which was opened by an old lady whose face was so familiar that it sent a shock through Doll's body. What had she expected, she asked herself: that time could change who you were? And then, before a word could be spoken, before the unanswerable questions could be asked, the old lady started to cry. "Arabella, I'm so glad you came."

"So am I," said Doll, whose path home had been blocked by pain. It had been easier to move in another direction, farther and farther, until it all faded behind her like smoke in the sky. "I'm so sorry…"

If only…

The alert had gone off at 8 p.m., and for eight terrifying hours, planes droned, bombs landed, and incendiaries burned on a slope until the all-clear sounded. Only when the sun had risen, and the fires had turned to embers, could the loss be seen. They found a soldier under a wall. A girl named Faith, a warden leaving the post, had her head blown off and hurled, with a savageness that seemed unthinkable, to a nearby street. One of life's foot soldiers, Faith was a skinny girl with big eyes and a crooked tooth she hid behind her hand when she laughed. Too young, too slight for such a hideous end.

Faith was Doll's cousin, and that horrible death on top of all the other horrors sent her into a state of shock that disguised itself as abandon, a shock that did not leave her for years, until after she had married Pepin and fled, she believed, like a thief in the night.

And now, she had waited too long and they were all dead. If she had told Snooks everything, he would have put her on that plane. *He* would have sent her home—to the low house with the red door—in time to make it right. Over the years, Doll had many doubts, but never for a moment did she question that brilliant day when she spotted Snooks in his grey suit and cocky hat with a smile as big as England. The thing about Snooks, the thing that lasted after he lost his hair, his strut, and his dashing demeanour, was his acceptance. Snooks never held anything against you, any weakness or admission; he just moved forward like Marciano in the ring and he took you with him.

The Houdini

When I joined the swim team, I was placed in the slow lane with a boy named Drew. "I can't dive off the blocks," he announced as though he was looking for an argument, "because my suit could fall off." Drew stared, measuring my response, standing so close that I could smell donairs on his wheezy breath.

Eyes concealed by goggles, I shrugged, and feigned blasé: "That's cool."

Drew pushed off the blue cement wall with an undulating *whooosshhhh* that sent a swell of wash into neighbouring lanes. Two little kids whooped as though a speedboat had passed, then flipped on their backs to ride out the wave, arms extended in Latin crosses. Awaiting my cue, I watched the pace clock.

"They don't put drawstrings in Speedos that large," the team's coach, Pammy, explained as Drew hurled himself down the lane, thumping, convulsing in an ungainly fly. He looked like a captive manatee hit with electrical shocks. His head jerked skyward, mouth open for air, a spasm of white-grey flesh. "I told him..." Pammy's voice trailed off, aimed more at herself than me. "It's going to be an issue on race day."

"Now go!"

Whenever Drew told you something excessive, he trapped you at the end of your lane, pressing so near in his voluminous mulberry Speedo that you squirmed. "Hey Rita, you probably heard that I had hernia surgery," he informed me after the set. I shrugged again. "It wasn't really a hernia," he declared with the imperious air of an only child. "It was a hydrocele, which is an abnormal swelling of the *scrotum.*" He cupped his hands in the shape of a Florida grapefruit, and sucked in air.

Because we lived in Myrtle, Nova Scotia, a minor town with modest expectations, the weekly newspaper covered our every undertaking: meets, bottle drives, Swim-A-Thons. One week earlier, a reporter had interviewed Drew, who boasted, without a hint of self-consciousness, "I like to play mind games in distance races," and the reporter, without a whiff of irony, printed it. When the story appeared, Drew's mother looked so proud of her son that I thought she might cry. Swim team was *my* mother's idea. There was no reason, declared Ethna, with a tenacious optimism that bordered on madness, that I could not become the best in the province or maybe the world.

Sports were not part of Myrtle's collective psyche. An Olympic rower visited my high school and students asked, "Have you tried bowling?" and "Is your brother a good dancer?"

The Myrtle Otters Swim Team (MOST) trained in the town's only pool, which had six lanes and a mural of frolicking dolphins wearing medals. We had forty swimmers, including twelve asthmatics, four kids with peanut allergies, and two boys who claimed, though they may have been lying, that they were legally blind. All of the girls were in love with Nathan Spearwater, the Otters' fastest swimmer, who at fifteen had dreamy eyes and abs. Ravaged by chlorine, his hair had hardened like points of meringue, which, in our minds, gave him a dangerous, yet vulnerable, air.

Before long I was promoted out of Drew's lane into the middle lane with Winston, Austin, a compulsive lane-puller, and Maura, whose father, Grant, was club president. A veteran of lumberjack competitions—his specialty was the hot saw—Grant had a long grey mullet and a mellow disposition. Mullets, best when curly and blond, are not as ridiculous as cynics think. In the eye of the wearer, the mullet creates the illusion of youth and glamour, preserving the golden locks that had once drawn praise from grandparents and doting moms, who gushed, at a time when you could do nothing else to distinguish yourself, "Oh, look at those curls. Aren't they beautiful?"

Substantial enough for a poultry plant and a hospital, Myrtle had all of the colours of a spring bouquet splashed on wooden houses. In a shady corner, where a boy from my school named Hubert MacLean lived, were flats and rental houses drained of pigment.

Our house was in a bouquet of modest bungalows, but what set it apart, my mother believed with the same conviction she applied to my swim career, was her flower garden. Every August, my family drove through Myrtle, assessing Ethna's rivals in the annual competition. Ethna, a five-time winner, had plump peonies as rich as vanilla ice cream, and hydrangeas so blue that they looked like a science experiment on osmosis.

"I don't like all the marigolds." I pointed to one yard. "Too hard and spiky."

"Nothing pleasing there," agreed Ethna, who not only avoided reds and yellows, but also harboured an abnormal hatred of sunflowers.

To Ethna, the gangly plants had an unsettling human quality. Like tanners, they turned their faces to follow the sun. They grew too tall, then collapsed, heads down like lynching victims. The anthropomorphic flowers had an eerie pattern of spiralling seeds, intricate enough to be named after a thirteenth century mathematician, and quite possibly a sign of something evil. The ominous plants had, in fact, possessed Van Gogh for an intense period before his tragic death.

"I am painting with the enthusiasm of a Marsellais eating bouilla-baisse," the Dutch artist wrote his brother from the south of France. "I am now on the fourth picture of sunflowers." Gold and yellow, the colours of God and the Sun, dying xanthic flowers, seed heads built up with impasto.

Ethna's competitiveness, rooted in a family of nine, extended past her garden to her children, whom she believed should be bigger and smarter than neighbouring offspring. That included the Kings, whose father was so tall that his licence plate said: BIGBOY.

Both my parents were of average size, but Ethna, ignoring the power of multiple and interacting genes, believed that the more we ate, the larger we would become. Like Moullard geese, funnel-fed three times a day, we were stuffed with fried chicken, tortillas, and cheesecake. To Ethna's delight, we did, for a while, grow tall and robust, surpassing our neighbours until the age of twelve, at which point we levelled off or succumbed to fat.

I was the fat one.

One day, Ethna and I saw a woman standing outside the poultry plant. Overhead, the sky was heavy with eagles, massive birds that roosted in trees and feasted on entrails left by farmers. Unknow-able creatures that could, to my surprise, swim.

The woman's grey hair was piled in a stack with loose strands drifting down the sides. Under a bulky coat, as formless as a judo jacket, was a trailing cotton skirt. She wore wire-rimmed glasses. Across her chest was a small cloth bag, covered with embroidery and sequins. It reminded me of pouches I'd seen in old cowboy movies, stuffed with gold.

The woman was staring into a void as she twirled a clump of loose hair around a finger. Over and over, systematically, as though the hair were endless.

"Who's that?" I asked Ethna.

"Lavinia MacLean. Hubert's mother."

"Really?" His mother, people said, was an artist. I squinted and split-screened Hubert and the woman, who didn't fit my mental image of an artist: angular, chic, dressed in black. Maybe this was why Hubert didn't have a home computer or a car, why he wore used clothes. "He's really bad at math," I added airily. "I wouldn't be surprised if he fails."

"I don't like that kind of talk." Ethna's jaw tightened with the same look I'd seen when Uncle Roger, the town denturist, strutted into rooms baring his teeth like a hyena. "Not everyone has the same advantages as you."

"I guess he has a really smart dog, though," I blurted, trying to recover. "They got him from the pound. His name is Scampy, and Hubert says he may enter him in a show."

"That's silliness," snapped Ethna, not to be tricked. "Silliness."

"Really! Hubert told Winston that his dog is related to a New-foundland dog who just won a medal for bravery from the Second World War."

"The Second World War?"

"That's what Winston said; that the dog was a hero."

That night, during practice, I ignored Drew, who was submerged at the bottom of his lane to hide from Pammy. During a tedious set of free, I contemplated the decorated dog, and I tried to visualize Scampy, whom I had seen from a distance, walking in the rain, head raised like he had something to be proud of.

Pammy enrolled us in a skills course being conducted by a city coach named Beluga, who had a voice like grinding gears. I hated Beluga and his swimmers. At one meet, they parked behind a turn judge, a dotty woman with failing vision, and amused themselves by prompting disqualifications. When one of us completed a turn, they gasped en masse and groaned, "Ohhhhhhhh noooo," suggesting a grievous infraction, which the judge, not wanting to look inept, noted. Beluga's pool was located in a neighbourhood of neck tattoos and knives. Once, when Pammy forgot to enter Austin in his races, he wandered away from the pool and got mugged outside a detox centre.

After the course, Pammy separated swimmers into lanes by stroke and distance. We added before-school practices, and every day, with a determination I had to admire, Ethna rose at 4:30 a.m. and drove me through the sleeping streets of Myrtle; a ritual that left us exhilarated and feeling, for a short but wonderful time, absolutely special.

The stands at our pool looked like a church balcony overhanging the lanes. Once inside, you were assaulted by chlorine and heat, a two-fisted attack that left you, after several hours, stupefied, unable to move.

During meets, I occasionally looked up and saw spectators: comatose, tongues extended, stripped to shorts or undershirts. Panting. The drug salesman who was always drunk and chewing gum; the senior who never knew where her grandson was because the parents had divorced and no one told her anything anymore. "Is Jimmy in this race?" she would bleat. "Is that Jimmy?" The parents of marginal kids who feigned disinterest by hiding behind books.

One day, I saw Ethna's sister, Irene, and her husband, Roger, in matching track suits. Roger's pockets were filled with business cards which he flicked at strangers as though he were dealing from a deck. *Roger O'Ball, licensed denturist. Wearing dentures is as natural as putting on socks in the morning and taking them off at night.* And then in emphatic font. **One in four Canadians can't be wrong.**

The O'Balls lived in a modern house with three floors and four baths. Positioned throughout the dwelling like Fabergé eggs were ashtrays made from dental impressions, all one-of-a-kind, according to Roger. Big mouths, crooked mouths, and one so small it had to be a child's. Always deferential, Irene put Roger in charge of the decorating. "No one in our family had style," she sighed to Ethna, as though it were a chromosomal burden like diabetes or colour blindness.

As teams filed out, Roger sat in the front row, judicious, studying the T-shirts: optimistic ones that urged *You Never Succeed Unless You Try*, or the combative *You Suck, So Suck It Up.* Our shirts invariably played on our acronym: *We Get The MOST Out Of Swimming.*

If you fill a lycra swim cap with water and hold it above someone's head, then let it drop, two out of three times, the hat will conform to the head. While everyone practised starts, Drew demonstrated the hat trick. I saw Roger frown, then point at Drew, who was wearing a T-shirt over his racing suit and a pair of winter boots.

The province's coaches held a meeting and decided that what was missing was: Fun. To rectify this, they resolved to use the word *fun* whenever possible: the Fun Relay, the Fun Eliminator. They gave meets fanciful names like The Iceberg Classic and The Spring Fever. "Studies show swimmers will not drop out," they announced with the forced grins of vacuum cleaner salesmen, "if they are having fun."

None of this mattered until they decided to introduce, at The Fall Gobbler, a fun event that became known among swimmers as

The Houdini. Using duct tape, coaches taped three batches of seven-year-olds together and pitched them into the pool. What was supposed to happen? I wondered as Beluga nodded his approval. Were the kids supposed to swim together? Or free themselves, then sprint?

Whatever the intent, it was like throwing a cat off a bridge in a bag. Thrashing, scratching, silent underwater panic. As the swimmers surfaced, their faces contorted in fear, a murmur spread through the crowd louder and louder until a lifeguard jumped in and grabbed a hysterical girl. "Moommmm-eeeeeeeeeee. Moommmmmm-eee," she choked.

Don't complain, I warned Ethna, don't complain, but someone did.

"If these parents have nothing better to do..." Pammy collapsed in a puddle of self-pity. Then, she miraculously arose, fighting through her tears with the same spunk that had characterized her swim career. Parents were both shamed and inspired. "Now Pammy, we *know* you are the expert!"

Pammy was five foot ten and broad-backed. In snapshots, she always had a can of Coca-Cola in one hand. Ethna said Pammy was dating a man named Rory Pottie because she had "missed her window of opportunity."

Rory wore his hair in an old-school brush cut. He was five foot five, though he invariably—even when standing nose to chest with mid-sized woman—claimed to be five nine. To compensate for his size, Rory had pursued a number of manly hobbies including bodybuilding and combat pistol shooting. He wore a leather jacket and threw out "hip" expressions like "straight up, buddy" and "right back at ya."

According to Ethna, every woman had a window and it was

small. Some squandered it on a man who dumped them after years of dating; others played the field too long. By then, the choices were meagre: misogynists, divorcees with kids, alcoholics. I thought about the crowd outside the detox centre where Austin had been mugged. One man had been watching a pack of YMCA joggers pass, shouting encouragement, "Good pace, lads, strong pace," and then, without warning, to an old man, who had fallen behind: "Pick it up, jackass!"

My window, I decided, would open after high school when I would join Weight Watchers and lose twenty-five pounds. Suddenly, men, like panhandlers, would be everywhere: in classes, at the bookstore. On the university team, I would meet Jeremy, a six-foot-four backstroker with bleached hair and a flawless nose. He would, not coincidentally, bear an eerie resemblance to Nathan, who had discovered during the summer he could do other sports, including rugby. "You traitor," we scolded. "You'll be back." When Nathan didn't come back, but did become a rugby star, we comforted ourselves with cheap insults. "Anyone can play rugby," we decided. "It's a goon sport."

When my aunt Gail was fifty, she took up running and won a lottery entry to the celebrated New York City Marathon. Gail was one of sixty thousand participants, including Kenyans and Ethiopians with wings instead of feet.

"Well, I hope she wins," offered Aunt Irene.

"She won't win," said Ethna, adjusting expectations.

"You don't know that," huffed Irene. "She might."

When Gail finished in under five hours, everyone looked miffed, as though she had failed them.

Pammy said we could not get fast unless we attended big meets in Ontario or Quebec, something she had earlier dismissed as a waste of money. Everyone signed on, including Georgina Vogel, who lived on a farm outside town. Georgina's whole family was slow; the kind of people described in empty obituaries as "kindhearted," and as a result, she was two grades behind in school. Georgina's brother wore a snowmobile suit and a thick black headband underneath a trucker's cap that said *Damn I'm Good*. He watched the movie *The Matrix* and, for six months, was terrified, believing it was real. Georgina had a lascivious side which made me uncomfortable; she called everyone—boys our age, parents, and teachers—"hotties." She often posed with her mouth half-open, tongue suggestively exposed like in a porno movie.

At the Ontario airport, we rented a van and drove to the pool, which was located in a sepia suburb of high rises and brick houses with pre-cast steps. Inside, you could imagine liquor cabinets and console TV sets topped with graduation photos. All of the brick looked left over from the construction of a jail, an asbestos-filled holding pen for drifters and drunks.

Overhead, the air was heavy with smog.

After our practice, Pammy drove us to a sandwich shop for supper. The area was morose, as though an enormous brown wind had blown through, leaving everything stained. I saw duplexes with undersized windows and lawn ornaments; I saw a short man driving a beater, wearing the same bandana as his two sullen toddler passengers.

Winston, who wore thick glasses, was ahead of me in the sandwich line. When Winston finished a race, he groped the deck for his glasses so that he could see the scoreboard and his time. On flip turns, I was always vigilant, wary of collisions.

"I'd like the roasted chicken *without* the sauce, please." Winston squinted.

"It comes with the ranch," growled the server, cutting the bread. Over her head was a sign that asked, as though they cared, *How Are We Doing?*

"But I don't want it, please."

She picked up a plastic bottle, looked at Winston, and squeezed a white line of sauce down the length of the sandwich. "It *comes* with the ranch."

In warm-up, all I could hear was the simultaneous splashing of ten lanes and the urgent "huuuppppp" of coaches. The brightly lit pool was cavernous, and when officials marched out, they wore blazers and ties.

At the massage tables, Pammy pointed out a muscular man who had been on the cover of the swim magazine I received in the mail. The man's name was Yorgo and he had flowing black hair and a permanent tan, unlike most of the swimmers, who seemed pale and bleached from chlorine. Yorgo could have been an Argentinean polo player with a Rolex and a Porsche and a thin, obscenely wealthy heiress who supported him and his one-hundred ponies until one day, in a jealous rage, she shot him dead. When Yorgo rolled over, I saw a maple leaf tattoo on his chest.

I stopped at the T-shirt stand where a man with a press would personalize your meet shirt with *Freestyle, Butterfly, Backstroke, Breaststroke,* or *IM*.

I was still thinking about Yorgo, who had, in my eyes, the elegance and passion of the tango, a man at home in an opera house or a throng of colourful pressed-tin houses. Yorgo would be magnanimous, I decided, knowing that success was *naturally* his and not something to be lorded over others. He would be gracious in victory, unlike the six-foot-tall girls who talked in stage voices about how embarrassing it would be to not make finals.

At home meets, Pammy wore a cowboy hat and ran down the side of the pool, screaming "go, go!" as though we were in a roundup. Sometimes, I imagined her on a palomino. If one of us had a good finish, Pammy would turn, find the parent in the stands, and beam, sharing in the feat. Here, in an unfamiliar pool that grew longer every day, a pool with stadium seats and an echo, Pammy sat immobile on the sidelines, sphinx-like with a can of Coke, race after race.

When I was in Grade Ten, we took metal shop in a drafty annex filled with squealing saws and power tools. "Now, don't touch that drilled metal," warned our teacher, who, ominously, had one arm. "It's extremely hot. It will burn you." Because Derald Murphy was an idiot and he was directly sitting behind me, I had no way of seeing him press the smoldering metal to my unprotected neck. As the teacher gasped and Derald tittered, I shivered in shock. Why? I wondered as my head whirled with pain. Because I was fat?

When things go badly at a swim meet, you pay for every sin of your life. Your time is flashed on the scoreboard and then pasted on a wall. There is no way to make the mortifying walk from the edge of the pool, wet and half-naked, to the dressing room, without someone asking disingenuously, "Oh, is she crying?" "Is she upset?" Through a gauntlet of Darwinian scorn, you dash, praying for your towel. Thighs rubbing. Stomach sucked in. Videotaped. In a calculated act of cruelty, your only true allies—your parents—are imprisoned in the stands where they cannot reach you.

"Why did you bother coming?" Pammy screeched at Georgina, who had her race numbers written down her arm in permanent marker. "*Why?*"

Gradually, on the pretext of seeking advice on scratches, Pammy panicked and abandoned us for the higher ground of Beluga and his star, a freestyler named Wren. When Wren won her heat, I saw Pammy turn to the stands, find the parents, and beam.

Still wearing my hat and goggles, I stumbled off deck past bodies and bags. I didn't think about my stash of energy bars; I didn't see the girls sucking on puffers, eyes closed like junkies. Somehow, I landed in the hallway, black and hollow as an elevator shaft, stripped of signs and inspirational posters, where I waited for my mind to stop racing like a rebooting disc. I tried not to think about finishing ninety-eighth in the one hundred Breast, about Austin's four DQs, about Beluga poking me in the stomach and saying, in his counterfeit voice, the one that dripped with fake wisdom, "You know what you have to do...," another poke, "to get faster." After an hour, maybe two, the team wandered out wearing T-shirts that improbably claimed: *Otters Have the MOST Fun in the Pool.*

Before we left for Ontario, Roger and Irene stopped by to wish us luck.

"Now, win some races for us," Irene grinned. I shrugged, armour in place, while Ethna, who dared to dream, twitched.

"It's a *very* big meet," Ethna started to explain.

"Oh you'll see," scoffed Irene, which was code for "We'll be checking the results." And then, before Ethna could protest further, Irene added, "Roger is hiring another assistant." I glanced at Roger, who had grown rich on the backs of toothless seniors and seasonal workers, mouths immortalized as ashtrays.

"Really?" Ethna asked.

Roger flashed his calling card: two rows of polymerized acrylic resin. When Roger smiled, he looked like someone who was caught rifling your medicine cabinet, a false, extravagant smile that suggested it was your fault, not his, that you'd caught him. "I need someone to handle the overflow," Roger announced. That smile, threatening and ugly as a stump fence.

Sounding high-minded for someone who'd spent the night at the motel ice machine filling buckets, Austin said he had not bought a meet T-shirt because he was saving four hundred dollars to get his cats' teeth cleaned. He had a picture of one of his cats wearing a hat made from an orange peel.

"Why?" asked Winston.

"Because no one else is going to do it," Austin answered. "Because *I* am not selfish."

Across the hall, I saw Grant admiring his mullet in a window; I saw him stoically smile at Ethna, who seemed in shock. At that moment, I wanted to tell Ethna about Hubert MacLean, who might be moving to another town. Winston said he'd met Scampy and the dog did seem extraordinary. Leashless, he walked by Hubert's side and couldn't be distracted by squirrels or cats, or a low-flying eagle that swooped from the sky like a malicious gryphon with Satanic powers. You could see, Winston argued, why Hubert would want to show him. Not for himself, but for the dog. When that show woman lectured him on pedigrees and papers, she proved how little she knew about life and love, and how little she knew about dogs, who don't need a war to save someone. Hubert, I decided, when I was wiser, should have kept Scampy under the pillow of his heart with all the things that gave him joy.

And then, before I could speak, I noticed a policeman questioning the president of the host club, a haughty woman from South Africa. Austin pointed. There was no way of getting around it, he declared, louder than necessary; someone *had* to be in trouble, and

it should be *her*. How could a fraud, an imposter with absolutely
no training, walk in off the street and massage swimmers for three
whole days? he demanded, as though he deserved an answer. Why
didn't she ask him for identification? What if he was a pedophile?

Maybe, Winston suggested, the story would make the newspaper.
Or the TV news. I was upset, I said, because the charlatan had
worked on Yorgo, who'd had a fabulous meet and didn't deserve to
be associated with something so sordid. Yorgo, Georgina snorted,
was "a hottie."

After four endless days, we felt a tenebrous relief, as though
something truly awful had happened, something that could
have—*should* have—been prevented. Something as witless as The
Houdini. It wasn't just relief, I admitted, as the woman threw up
her hands. It was the same *schadenfreude* we had felt when Drew
dove off the blocks and his suit fell down; the same joy I had seen
on Irene's face, when she realized, long before Ethna, that I was
hopeless. An emotion so potent and primal that it must, some
clerics preached, be the devil's work. And it was all around us, as
eerie as sunflowers in the south of France.

Wishing Well

Cameron was about five foot six, but seemed smaller. He blamed his tiny frame on his parents, a former priest and a nun, who were in their late forties when he was born. In their new lives, free from the vows of poverty and chastity, the parents had become avid curlers, embracing the clubby atmosphere and light-hearted tippling they had missed in their consecrated lives. Their car had a bumper sticker that said *Curling, Can You Hack It?* They had yearly tickets to the Brier.

Cameron and his parents spent most of their spare time at Pineville Curling Club, an unobtrusive building in the shadow of an oil refinery. The club had six sheets of ice, a bar, and a gift shop, where you could purchase, in the weeks leading up to Christmas, earrings shaped like brooms.

Cameron bought his mother a Styrofoam hat formed like a stone; he bought his father a T-shirt that boasted *My Drinking Team Has a Curling Problem.*

Both of Cameron's parents were in the bar drinking rye and gingers the night he suffered his first concussion, an event that changed the course of his life.

"Oh no," Cameron's mother gasped as she ran down the stairs and onto the ice where the teen lay prone, arms splayed as though he had been shot. "Somebody get help."

A doctor hustled down, and was informed along the way that Cameron was plagued by bad balance, a baffling condition that caused him to crash to the ice whenever he slid out of the hack.

Sometimes, the fall was preceded by a vain attempt at recovery; on other occasions, Cameron toppled over like a fainting goat.

"I think it's his inner ear," Cameron's mother suggested, while Dennis, Cameron's surly skip, rolled his eyes.

Dennis believed that Cameron's bad balance was psychological: Cameron could not envision himself as a winner and fell in a form of self-sabotage. Others speculated that the poor balance was caused—not by a late release—but by his older parents, who had left their miracle baby so "high strung" that he became nauseous before tournaments. Or maybe, some conceded, he was born unsteady.

"It's a Grade One concussion," the doctor concluded. "Watch him for twenty-four hours."

Cameron's room was decorated in a curling motif with posters and an ice bucket shaped like a stone. For his twenty-third birthday, his parents had bought him a minifridge which he used for energy drinks and beer. He had an Xbox 360 and a computer.

At one point in his life—in that vague period between school and work—he had gone through a rebellious phase, wearing a Columbine coat and a leather choker. He had attached handcuffs to his belt loops and listened to Slayer. He was also addicted to online gambling for two years, but had kicked the habit.

"What are you doing?" his mother asked.

"Watching the video again." He nodded to the TV, at the shady image of an icemaker crossing the ice.

"He makes it look so easy," she noted.

"He always does," replied Cameron, who could hear—in the uncanny silence of their house—his father snoring.

Cameron had reset his goals after his third concussion. Instead of becoming a world-class skip with trophies and groupies and a patented slider, he would become *The Ice Master*, the finest icemaker in the country. "The balance thing was a blessing," explained Cameron, who had rejected his mother's suggestion that he wear a hockey helmet while curling. "Icemaking isn't just a dream. It's my calling."

To fulfill his dream, Cameron was saving money to travel from his home in New Brunswick to Wishing Well, Saskatchewan, where he could apprentice at the feet of the Number Three icemaker in the country, Wally Watavinsky. Number Two was an alcoholic. Number One, a steely-eyed Austrian named Gunther, was temperamental and prone to fits of rage when faced with rising humidity or faulty water lines, but Number Three was perfect. On the grainy video, Cameron watched Watavinsky walk down the ice backwards, waving a wand back and forth like a priest with a censer on a chain.

Barb Batterman was Pineville Curling Club's star.

A curling icon in her late forties, Barb was known for her daring takeouts and ferocious style. On the ice, she wore a zipped polyester windbreaker and black unisex slacks. Barb's slacks were cut like a policeman's uniform and she walked with a macho cop swagger. Barb was often described as "feisty" and "combative," adjectives applied in place of loftier titles, such as Heart Champion or Olympian, which were beyond her reach.

After years of hearing the descriptions, Barb had become a caricature of herself. At a tournament in Wisconsin, she let the door slam in the face of a competitor following her into the washroom. She spit on the ice. She started wearing a ball cap backwards and tried chewing tobacco. She got a man's haircut and became one of those curious figures like Pat on *Saturday Night Live*, an odd genderless being—only this time with an edge.

Barb's husband was the primary caregiver to their only child, a confused teen who called herself a vegan and a member of the animal liberation movement. While Barb divided her days between her job as a safety inspector and her career as a curling personality, Amanda sent threatening emails to a medical school and riding stables. "Release the horses by noon on Friday or be prepared for dire consequences. This is not a joke!"

Sometimes, with palpable pity, neighbours offered Amanda drives. "Is your mother away curling?" they would ask the rain-soaked child, who felt asphyxiated by Barb's tremendous ego and had developed a habit of closing her eyes when people spoke to her. It had started around the time that Barb introduced, at competitions, her low fist pump, a gesture that divided aficionados: Was it too much, some wondered, or just Barb being Barb?

Amanda had learned to make herself invisible during the curling season, when Barb vacillated between periods of silence and hysterical sobbing. The mood swings had been addressed by a sports psychologist, who instructed Amanda to move the television into her bedroom and to put her cellphone on vibrate. "Intensity," he argued, "is your mother's most lethal weapon."

It was 7 p.m. and Cameron watched Barb guide a man in an ultrasuede jacket into the club bar. Barb spoke in one of those female jock voices, a contrived voice with the inflection of an air traffic controller.

"I play the game hard and that's all I know," Barb boasted.

"That's what makes you a winner," her guest chortled back.

The man was Billy Joe Cunningham, Barb's main sponsor and the owner of Sizzle, a popular steak house. For years, Billy Joe had been saddled with the nickname *Maudie* because of his resemblance to Maudie Frickert, the randy old lady Jonathan Winters played in drag. Billy Joe hated the nickname. Barb addressed him as Billy Joe in a loud voice when she attended the Sizzle Christmas party, where she ate hors d'oeuvres and shared her winning philosophy with the kitchen staff.

"How long can you keep it up?" asked a line cook.

"As long as it's still fun."

"That's the girl," laughed Billy Joe.

Everyone knew that Barb would play and play until she could no longer win and then announce, as though anyone believed it, that she was retiring to "spend time with my family," who by then would be fully grown. Barb deposited Billy Joe in the bar where he could glance at the scoreboard between rum and cokes. After making her final shot, Barb slid down the ice and surreptitiously smacked her broom against her leg, dislodging a nearly invisible scatter of debris—just enough to alter the course of a shot.

Billy Joe left the bar and Cameron's former skip, Dennis, arrived.

After Cameron had retired from curling, Dennis had become a provincial junior champion, an accomplishment he had lorded over Cameron for years. When Dennis's curling rise later stalled, he quit mid-season, blaming Osgood-Schlatter disease, a knee affliction that can accompany growth. Only after everyone's expectations had been lowered to a more comfortable level had the former prodigy returned to the ranks.

"How's the icemaking coming?" Dennis joined Cameron.

"Good," Cameron nodded. "I'm probably going to Sask this year."

"Sask is cold as hell, man."

"New Brunswick winters aren't much better."

"You're probably right."

Cameron had researched Wishing Well, and he knew that the average winter temperature was minus twenty Celsius, a detail that seemed insignificant in the grand scheme of things. Wishing Well was a curling oasis that greeted visitors with a billboard of native son Curt Koharski, world junior champion. The town had a retro fifties feel with ball diamonds, picnic tables, and an outdoor pool with a shower. Cement animals on springs. For nature lovers, it boasted sharp-tailed grouse and ring-necked pheasants. Outside town, you could savour the stillness of the prairie, a bald expanse once roamed by buffalo, now silent save for the footsteps of deer and the rustle of grass. Sixty kilometres away was a ghost town.

Cameron had also Googled Wally, who had strong views on the double vs. single hack conundrum. Wally had staunch supporters who leapt to his defence online if critics dared to call his ice frosty or slow. On one curling forum, a man with the username Knock Your Rocks Off threw down: "I consider Vink a personal friend, and challenge any man who calls his ice picky."

The response from Teflon Tim: "Maybe if Vink spent less time in the bar and with the ladies, curlers would have a higher percentage."

Knock Your Rocks Off: "Shows how well you know Vink."

Under the tutelage of Wally, Cameron would master the hygrometer and the art of pebbling; he would learn to flood to perfection. When great men see their future, they see themselves in *that* moment: on the podium, in the presidential office, and all of the inconsequential clutter of life is missing. Cameron could see himself in the Extra End Bar being toasted by curlers. He could envision himself travelling to Japan, where the cab drivers wore ties and white gloves, and he could see the Canadian rink—which claimed never to have lost on "good ice"—closing their eyes in relief when he entered the building. "Thank God. He's here."

❀   ❀   ❀

Cameron's mother entered his room. She looked around, mindful of an incident a few years back. While walking home from his job at the liquor store, Cameron had spotted a CD on the sidewalk outside the high school. He slipped it in his bag. It had been a reflex, an involuntary action like shielding your face at a hockey game when a puck takes flight, and by the time he had reconsidered, he was the owner of *Thug Life: Vol. 1* by Tupac Shakur.

Days later, while collecting dirty laundry, Cameron's mother found the CD. She felt relieved. This was proof, she decided, that he *was* in touch with popular culture, that he *did* have interests of his own, that they had not made him "different."

After that, on every special occasion, Cameron received a Tupac-related gift: books, CDs, posters, and even obscure academic papers supporting the conspiracy theory or the more radical notion that Tupac—or Makaveli—was alive. "*Tupac Resurrection* is going to be on television tonight," Cameron's mother noted one evening. "You know it was nominated for an Academy Award. I'm sure it's worth seeing again."

Cameron's mother had the gentle voice of a hospital volunteer, one of those ladies named Margaret or Bette or Dot. White-haired women in pastel smocks, who had seen enough of life to remain stoic when the ambulance attendants raced by with a crash victim, the mangled remains of someone's son or daughter, the end of a life.

She was holding the newspaper. "Did you see this?" she asked. "Vandals spray-painted Sizzle. They wrote words like *Killers* and *Inhumane Butchers* on the walls."

She looked at Cameron as though he should have a response.

"Isn't that Barb's sponsor?" she asked.

"Yeah," shrugged Cameron, ambivalent. "It is."

Days before someone had spray-painted Sizzle, Barb Batterman, that celebrated force of ego and determination, had been locked in her bedroom sobbing. "What's wrong?" asked her husband, who then phoned her sports psychologist, a dour man named Theo, who brushed by Barb's family as though they had done something horrendous.

"How is she?" asked Ollie, the husband, when Theo emerged from Barb's room.

Theo did not answer, choosing instead to glare at Amanda, who closed her eyes, becoming invisible. "It is essential," he told the teen, "for you to have as little contact with your mother as possible until provincials are over. She has to visualize her success."

Barb's success was—according to Theo—based on her refusal to lose, as well as her uncanny ability to block out distractions: a questionable claim given what had happened two days earlier at a Toronto airport. Barb had been returning from a tourney. She was holding a trophy case when she became fixated on a tall young man with stubble. He was wearing jeans and a grey T-shirt—as though anything more would have been superfluous—and on his shoulders was a young Asian girl. There was no need to accessorize his outfit, Barb realized, when he had added this child, this serene child who seemed accustomed to her lofty position. They made such an impact, towering above the overdressed, the impatient, the self-consciously fat, that Barb moved closer until she saw the delicate woman beside them in a black top and pants. Barb decided the family was flaunting their good looks in their minimalist attire, making it seem so effortless, exuding an aura she found disturbing.

Barb stiffened in the oversized plaid tam she was wearing. In a rare self-deprecating act, in a vain attempt at showing the ferocious Barb Batterman having "fun," Barb had donned the goofy hat, topped with a pompom, and mugged for the cameras at the curling rink. The crowd had laughed. And Barb had almost forgotten about the buxom blond named Inge who had stolen everyone's attention while Barb was making her final takeout, hitting like a guided missile. Inge in the short plaid skirt and tight sweater, Inge with her hair in braids like a schoolgirl vixen.

Barb—the embodiment of competiveness—glared at the family, so Zen-like, so harmonious, that they *had* to be smug, they *had* to be judgmental, and then the mother took a cloth from her pocket and wiped the girl's face so gently, so lovingly, that Barb's psyche began to unravel.

Wally Watavinsky ruptured his spleen when he slammed his pickup into a grain silo. It happened on the same day that Barb's husband found two cans of spray paint in Amanda's closet: fluorescent green, and the red of slaughtered animals. There was also a brochure for Sizzle with discount coupons attached. Ollie and Amanda opened the computer's email, and together deleted eight messages threatening to stage an open rescue at a chicken farm and to firebomb a horse stable. "We won't tell your mother," Ollie promised.

Cameron was debating whether to tell his mother about his recent bouts of bad balance and the fall he had suffered at the club. That morning, he had watched his mother in the kitchen, struck, for the first time, by how much she had aged. Her hair was white, and she was moving slowly, rationing her movements as though she did not know how many she had left. She picked up a piece of cheese, studied it, and returned it to the fridge.

"Did you have a good time with Dennis?" she asked.

"Yeah, it was all right," he allowed.

"That's nice," she replied with too much enthusiasm.

Cameron's mother volunteered at a hospice; she took baskets of food to poor people in a housing project. She was still serving God, still wracked by guilt, the profound Catholic instilled in her since childhood. All the while, she feared that her son—the only child of older parents—might not fit in. Dennis was proof, she now decided, that Cameron had his own life, that he was not smothered by her good intentions and boundless love.

Cameron was thinking about Dennis, who after consuming six beers had confessed that he hadn't really suffered from Osgood-Schlatter. He just couldn't handle losing. Cameron, in turn, told Dennis that his last concussion was a Grade Three injury which may have left him with a permanent disability.

"No shit," said Dennis, who seemed to think he owed Cameron something. "I don't know if I should tell you this..."

"What?"

"Wally and Barb..."

About ten years ago, explained Dennis, Wally Watavinsky had been snowed in during a bonspiel in Bismarck, North Dakota. It had been a trying day, with Americans griping about bad ice. After six hours in the bar, Wally was so loaded and so bored that he hooked up with Barb Batterman, who, in an attempt to appear alluring, had applied teal eye shadow and hair gel that smelled like melons. Wally was a ladies' man, so it wasn't surprising that he smiled, not cruelly but with a touch of amusement, when Barb offered to leave her husband.

"Are you sure, man?" asked Cameron.

"Oh yeah," Dennis confirmed. "Vink was hard up that night, but he was man enough to recover."

"Wow."

"It's all good, though," Dennis told him. "There's a hot blond named Inge who likes him. *A lot!*"

Cameron could have been disappointed, he could have been disgusted, but he was, in fact, relieved. The tawdry story was enough to answer the voice in his head, the one that told him that he needed to move, he needed to be more, he needed to make his parents proud.

After Cameron had parted with Dennis, he had taken a cab to a bar filled with pool tables. He saw a grizzled man in a hunting jacket. Two junkies. Cameron's pulse quickened as he approached a room at the back, and when he settled onto a bar stool, he looked like a man who had received a clean biopsy report. It was a look of reckless freedom and emancipation. Cameron slid twenty dollars in the VLT, erasing the aftertaste life had left in his mouth. Cameron spent his entire paycheque, and when he bustled from the bar in a euphoric mood, he was weightless.

Cameron's mother was talking now, and her voice felt like layers of bubble wrap, and at that moment, Wishing Well *was* a dream, an imaginary oasis with an outdoor pool and cement animals on springs, as mythical as Zerzura, the whitewashed desert city. Cameron looked around his room, at his curling pin collection, at his baptism candle. An old Slayer poster: *God hates us.*

"They say that Wally was drinking," his mother said.

"He usually is," said Cameron.

"That's terrible," she clucked as though they had written the dialogue together. "He will kill himself or someone else the next time."

Through his walls, Cameron could smell cabbage rolls, his favourite meal.

"Are you tired, dear?" His mother placed a hand on his forehead as though she was checking his temperature or warding off demons. Cameron closed his eyes and sighed.

Finbar

My brother is a totally awesome surfer. He entered an event called the International Cup last year, competing against guys from New Jersey and Virginia, and came third overall, which makes him the best in Nova Scotia. He has sweet moves: cutbacks, airs, and 180s. I've seen him do some filthy stuff.

He used to be a swimmer, but he quit after six years in an eight-lane fifty-metre pool. Back and forth, back and forth. My parents put him in swimming because they thought he was hyperactive, and when he quit, they blamed his coach, Dee Dee, for ending his Olympic dreams. I think he just wanted to get outside and do something dangerous.

Whenever I went to his meets, it was stinking hot and the chlorine made my head hurt. Everyone had a stopwatch and looked extremely tense. One woman kept shouting "Go Mah-reeee-ahhh! Go!" at a horrible pitch.

Coach Dee Dee was okay, but childish. If you got a best time, you were supposed to pick out a sticker and paste it on a board. Most of the stickers were animals: bears, pigs, and chickens. The older boys would try to get two pink pigs, which they would stick on top of each other like the pigs were doing something rude. Eventually, Dee Dee would see them and run across the deck screaming, "Move that pig, move that pig." It was funny because Dee Dee was knock-kneed and ran with her hands out at her sides.

❀ ❀ ❀

I'm small for fourteen and my hair is bright blond and fried. The first time my brother took me surfing, he left me in the parking lot while he talked to friends. I was jammed up in my neoprene wetsuit when two old folks shuffled by. The man, who was using a cane, sized me up, and announced in a Scottish brogue, "Ahhh, a surf smurf." I thought that was rich for a dude his age.

You see all kinds at the beach: old dudes, wannabes, real surfers like my brother. I always see these two women with boards. Doughy, they're in their thirties. One has a humongous tattoo of an eagle on her back, but it's sketchy like a prison tattoo with no solid colour or definition. In her street clothes, she looks like a person who collects water samples for the government and reads books about witches. Sometimes, she smiles at my brother.

My brother started university in Halifax last year, which, in his mind, makes him a big shot. One day he brought home a new friend from school. Elliott had long black hair, and looked like Mowgli from *Jungle Book* if Mowgli wore ice-blue Oakleys. Elliott had an iPod Photo and a Mac PowerBook with a seventeen-inch screen.

"His father is a wealthy Japanese businessman," said my brother, who watches too much TV.

The way he said it, you immediately imagined a slick man in a business suit who was either shutting down a car factory in Michigan or ordering up a hooker and getting murdered in his fancy hotel.

"You sound stupid," I told my brother, who grinned.

I need my brother for drives because he has a licence and I'm too young to drive. Sometimes, he picks me up at school. Because I'm blond and he's dark, people think we are stepbrothers, but we aren't.

My brother loves to hear about my science class with Mr. Clahane, who is always leaving the room and disappearing in the building for thirty minutes. Occasionally, the principal will notice his absence and go on the PA system: "Would Mr. Clahane please return to his classroom?" Five minutes later: "Would Mr. Clahane please return to his classroom?" And then: "Would a representative of Mr. Clahane's class come to the office?"

Most times, nobody bothers.

One day, Mr. Clahane brought in a walkie-talkie. Then, he left. Danny and Josh picked it up and started talking to a highway construction site, where the foreman was giving directions to a worker at the top of a hill.

"Get off our channel!" the foreman ordered.

"No," replied Danny.

"We know where you are."

"We know where *you* are."

"We are going to call the police."

"We *are* the police."

My brother thought it was funny.

I got my own board for Christmas: a Bic Mini Malibu, a good starter board. Because Elliott can afford anything, including the most notorious board, my brother got him into surfing. Elliott has his own apartment, a flat screen TV, and an American Express card that he uses for whatever he wants.

Elliott owes my brother, who talked him out of this incredibly stupid plan. Elliott was going to drop out of college, not tell his parents, and spend the second term's tuition at Cyclone's Pro Wrestling Academy, which teaches not only the art of pro wrestling, but ring psychology and business skills. He got the idea from watching court TV, where two soft-looking guys told the judge they

had met on the "independent wrestling circuit." Intrigued, Elliott
went on the Internet and found Cyclone's. My brother told Elliott
he could buy a Channel Islands board shaped by Al Merrick for the
same money. He showed him the movie *Riding Giants;* he told
Elliott that Laird Hamilton was married to the hottest woman
athlete in the world. Six foot three, she used to be an outrageous
volleyball player, and then a supermodel.

People think my brother could be a model even though he has crazy
eyes and a gnarly scar on his arm. People still want to be around him.
They like the way he moves, the way he talks. I'm more quiet.

My brother cracks up when I tell him about my school. Last
year, a dude named Sherman got an entire page in the yearbook
with pictures and a poem because they thought he was dead. *In
Memoriam,* it said. Sherman is in my law class this year, where the
same two guys slouch in their seats every class, wearing G-Unit
clothes. Whenever the teacher explains something, they interrupt
as though they're experts, starting every sentence with: "When I in
court..."

The teacher brought up jurors, and they growled, "They
snitches."

"No, Lorando, jurors are *not* snitches."

"They snitches."

My mother is always going on about how bad the schools are. I
don't tell her the worst stuff. One of the teachers eats erasers
because of stress. Lorando stabbed a guy and did six months in the
youth centre. When Lorando's cousin was killed in a crackhouse,
his mother told the newspaper he was a "stay-at-home dad who
liked to draw," and the paper printed it. My father believes it's all a
neo-con conspiracy to erode the schools. I don't get his point.

My parents don't know about all of the dangerous stuff my
brother does. He jumped off a cliff; he skateboards through traffic.
They think he's mellow because he listens to Jack Johnson. I'm not
supposed to tell them that my brother quit swimming because some

coach accidentally "bumped" him in the shower and my brother punched his face.

He might have quit anyway. If you put a dolphin in a space like that, a small chlorinated pool, he can get depressed, diseased, and eventually die. That's what the animal rights people say.

My mother's big fear is that my brother will drop out of school and move to Alberta. The newspaper is full of ads for welders, oilfield workers, or kitchen help. My mother once saw a story in the newspaper about a Brad Pitt movie in Alberta. Pitt was playing a cowboy who had nine fingers, and when the producers went looking for a hand double—someone with a missing finger—they found them everywhere.

"What does that tell you," she asked, "about how safe it is?"

My brother ignores my mother. He thinks he's clever with words. Whenever we play poker, he says stuff like "By the time you're finished, all you'll have left is chump change."

"You sound stupid," I tell him, and he grins.

Last year, despite his stupid jokes, he took me winter surfing, which was awesome. After Christmas, when the temperature hits minus twenty Celsius, the crowd gets small. The best storms are in early winter when you need gloves, boots, and hoods, but still get brainfreeze. Sometimes, hard-core surfers come from California for the hurricanes that churn up seaweed and turn the water brown. They sleep in their vans and have names like Scooter or Love. They have the best boards and sponsors.

One Saturday, we went to the beach. The day had started off weird because first I ran into Mr. Clahane in a department store with a dumpy woman who had two little kids dressed in costumes. In the lineup for photos, the kids were crying. One was a rabbit, the other a fairy princess. "Stop it," the woman scolded the rabbit who looked at me like he wanted help. "You know you like getting your picture taken." And then to Mr. Clahane, who pretended he didn't see me, "They *really* do."

The sky at the beach was the colour of concrete; there were two-metre waves and a touch of rain. Some goofs on skimboards were blasting down the beach; a tourist asked my brother to pose with her in a picture. By supper time, everyone was gone except for me, my brother, and Elliott, who was learning moves.

The coming storm must have affected my brother because he got all philosophical about surfing, which he never does. He told Elliott about Duke Kahanamoku, a notorious surfer and talented swimmer nicknamed The Human Fish. According to the legend, Duke rode a ten-metre wave caused by an earthquake in Japan.

My brother's personal goals were "to enjoy the beauty of life, to awake each day happy, to become the human being I was meant to be."

"You sound stupid," I told him, and he grinned.

And then I saw him: a stranger on a wave.

As the stranger pulled a clean cutback, I wondered: *Where the heck did he come from?* Not the empty parking lot, not the deserted beach. Everyone had left, including the woman with the eagle tattoo, who, on her way to the beach, had bought a rhubarb pie at a roadside stand and eaten the whole thing.

The stranger was tanned, with hair to his shoulders and knots beneath his knees. He sat on the wet sand and stared at the ocean which was roaring like a plane. I'm not as good at describing stuff as my brother, but just let me say, the ocean takes all of your concentration. When you are there, you can't think about school or money or the future. The ocean is a cold, hard gauntlet pounding you from all sides. The salt stings your eyes, the sand swirls under your toes, and you feel like the Earth is giving way and you are free-falling to a place you've never been, a place you can't imagine.

My brother tapped the stranger's back. The sand beneath him smelled like seaweed and decomposed fish. When the guy turned, he had the weirdest look I've ever seen. It was like someone who was listening, in his head, to an amazing song he'd written by himself.

"Are you done?" my brother asked.

"Yeah," he said.

"Where's your ride?"

The guy pointed to his board.

"Where are you from?"

He pointed at the roaring ocean.

"Where do you crash?"

He looked around the beach and shrugged. "Here?"

That's how he ended up living at Elliott's apartment. The surfer said that whenever he went someplace new, some place he didn't understand, he let the people there name him. That way he became reborn, part of the local fabric. Elliott suggested Washi, which means eagle in Japanese. My brother said that I was good at naming cats so I should pick the name. I was going to go with a surf name like Kelly or Duke or maybe Sunshine, but then I thought about this show I'd seen on TV about three Irish tenors. In their black suits, the tenors seemed mysterious like they could have been spies or IRA hitmen.

"Finbar," I said. "It means white-haired."

Everyone nodded and my brother grinned, "That's tight, man, that's tight."

Finbar says they're going to go to Maui to find Jaws, which has twenty-five-metre waves and tow-in surfing. It's epic, he said, and my brother nodded. Elliott told his father that tuition jumped four K, and his father believed him. Now, he's emptying his bank account and selling all his stuff. I'm not supposed to tell my parents, and if I don't, Elliott will buy me the sweetest board I've ever seen, probably a Channel Islands, and maybe an intermediate one because I can catch waves now and turn pretty good. A board like that could change my life.

The Teddy Bears' Picnic

Normal sniffled. The air was still smoky from an overnight garage fire, the third suspicious blaze in Chatterville that month.

"I hates dat smoke," griped Normal, whose bushy hair had receded to a cul-de-sac.

"Me too," said Goose, thin and worn as an old bike tire.

Normal was a school bus driver, and Goose his unpaid assistant. Normal squinted and shuffled his thoughts like a deck of Crazy Eights. He stretched his legs, which had—weeks after his thirty-sixth birthday—turned orange, the same tint as the tators he purchased each payday. Normal was wearing his name tag, the one that stated *Hello, My Name is Normal.*

Minutes after their morning run, the two men were sitting on a lawn. From their vantage point, they could survey the elementary school that their passengers attended. Normal spotted a tardy student arriving on foot. Cradling a teddy bear, the girl was drifting by a white clapboard house with frothy sheers. By the time she had floated to the crosswalk, Normal was there, stepping into traffic, hand raised like a protestor's placard.

"Tell Mrs. Bonang to save me some cookies from da Teddy Bears' Picnic," he ordered, as he stomped the girl across the street. "She knows what kinds I like."

Normal had taken over the driver's job after Earl, a longhair in a leather ball cap, had crashed the bus into an oak tree, dislodging the bottle of Smirnoff's stored under his seat. Earl's crash and the subsequent discovery of the vodka had horrified Mrs. Bonang, the emotionally delicate primary teacher, who was relieved when Normal assured her he was a teetotaller. Grateful, Mrs. Bonang baked him a birthday cake. "Normal, don't ever think we take you for granted," she gushed. "You are our guardian angel."

Normal smiled at the memory of the cake, and then sang, almost to himself: "If you go down in the woods today, you're sure for a big surprise."

Mrs. Bonang's school was two blocks away from Champlain University, the town's principal employer. Five thousand students attended the school known for its liberal arts program and loyal alumni. Normal belonged to the university Booster Club and had, for three years running, been named Top Salesman in the popcorn fundraiser.

He was on a first-name basis with the owner of the vegetarian cafe—Artichokes and Friendly Folks—as well as the counter server at the all-night pizza parlour. He knew the manager of Cricket Lane Books, who lent him weighty books he could not read. It could be argued that Normal knew everyone in Chatterville, a town of pep rallies and poetry readings. A political pet who crossed party lines as freely as he switched highway lanes, Normal surfaced at election victory parties, where he hugged the winner as though they'd been separated at birth. "Oh that Normal," people would gush, democratic socialism validated. "*He's* involved in everything!"

Normal had a treat box on his bus; parents kept it filled with goodies. He had a gumball machine. On hot days, he allowed the boys to ride with their heads out the windows. Earl had forced the students to stay in their seats; he confiscated the Bic lighters they used to burn holes in the seat backs, and he departed each stop on time. Normal waited for stragglers and parents rewarded him with candy.

One hour after his morning run, Normal was still on the lawn. He could feel the familiar storm building his head, a low-pressure area fuelled by strange thoughts and urges, spiralling inward, crackling like the static on a TV screen. Noting Normal's mood, Goose tried to distract him by pointing at the book Normal had dropped on the grass.

"What's dat?"

"Dat's da word of God. If I reads it, the Church Lady says we can come to her house for supper."

"Yeah?"

Goose knew the Church Lady and her son, who worked at the recycling plant. The boy, named Arthur, had told Goose that he dreamed of killing his father, who had abandoned his family for a hairdresser named Bianca. His mother, Arthur said, was "a fool." The Church Lady spent most of her time visiting Chatterville's temporary shelter in search of converts, lost sheep who could, with the grace of God, be saved.

Normal shuffled to the corner to pick up a stray dime. When he returned, he blinked like someone surfacing from a dunk tank. Goose looked drained, unable to support the weight of his huge Fu Manchu and Normal's shifting mood.

If you go down in the woods today, you're sure for a big surprise." Normal was singing while he drove. He geared down the bus as the road narrowed and the houses shrunk like flowers in the shade. They were on their way to the Church Lady's house. It was bleak out here in the sticks, beyond the glow of Champlain University and its illuminating references to Basquiat and the chaotic reality of city life, deaf to cryptic jokes about the metaphysical chicken. Out here, refrigerators slouched on doorsteps, and long-haul truckers with skewed body rhythms came and went while dogs roamed the woods for game.

"It's hot here in da rhubarbs." Normal adjusted his glasses, which were so thick that jokers from the high school had nicknamed him Bulletproof. On a bad day, Normal looked like something the dog had choked up, a masticated ball of gristle and fat.

Years ago, when the area was nothing but woods, Normal's father had borrowed a car and driven the family to a roadside ice cream stand. Beside the stand was a wooden cage containing two raccoons. On slow days, people made the drive just to see Buzz and Bucky, who had coarse hair and black bands around their eyes. They moved about their enclosure with a flat-footed bear walk, and they dunked their food in water to everyone's amusement. One day, after feeding the raccoons, the owner accidentally left the cage's wire door ajar, and Buzz, who weighed twenty-five pounds, broke loose and—in a move that stunned everyone—bit a woman's leg so deeply, she needed fourteen stitches.

Normal laughed out loud.

Normal, who had attended receptions at the Champlain president's house, was disappointed. The Church Lady's living room, he decided, smelled like a blind, incontinent dog. He studied the artwork on the walls: a series of family portraits taken in a department store. Over the years, the Church Lady's appearance was unchanged, whereas just before he bolted, Arthur's father had had a poodle perm.

"He was born dead," Normal told the Church Lady, pointing at Goose.

"Really?" She looked at Goose.

"Dat's why he's not right."

"That's God's will, Normal, God's will."

Goose had worked, for twenty-two years, at a service station where he was a constant in rainstorms and blizzards: pumping gas, washing windshields, and checking oil, until one day he found a lump on his neck. By the time his chemotherapy had ended, all of the gas pumps had been converted to self-serve, and Goose's job was gone. For a while, he lived in a culvert.

Arthur entered the room, scowling. The Church Lady beamed at the boy, a forced smile that refused to see the darkness.

"Arthur helps with the chores and he has a job at the recycle plant," she said.

Arthur muttered something about "cheap fuckers" just as the phone rang and the Church Lady excused herself. "I'm livin' in the ass end of space," moaned Arthur as he plopped into a threadbare chair and pulled out a smoke. In the room, the air was damp and disappointed; nail heads popped through the Gyproc, as desperate to escape as Arthur.

Normal picked at a plate of soggy crackers, wondering when dinner would be served. His stomach growled, and his head began to crackle. As Goose filled his pocket with grapes, Normal looked at Arthur, who had a CROOKS tattoo on one arm.

Arthur looked back, and asked: "You wants in on something?"

"Sure," Normal wheezed.

The Church Lady returned and fixed her eyes upon her sullen son. "Arthur, have you been sharing God's word?"

"I'm bousta do dat," said Arthur, who had only seen gangstas on TV.

"Pardon me?"

"Yes, I have."

❀   ❀   ❀

On their way to meet Arthur, Normal and Goose ambled down Main Street. They passed the fire station, which had assigned pagers to its volunteers after the third suspicious fire. One block later, Normal spotted Professor Bilby, a regular popcorn customer, washing his Volvo wagon in his driveway. Everything about Bilby was impeccable; from his car to his house, a heritage property with four fireplaces and a Dutch oven. Cambry House, they called it, in a town that liked to christen its landmarks and unabashedly boast "the most educated populous in the province."

Before he retired from Champlain University, Professor Bilby had occupied a corner office overlooking a contemplative courtyard. His area of expertise was post–WWI Germany and he had, for a while, immersed himself in the greed and depraved sensuality of a decaying society. Drawn to the decadence, Bilby visited Berlin and the dark alleys of Lustmord; he covered his walls with grotesque Otto Dix portraits of crippled veterans and garish whores until it became too real.

"Hallo, Mr. Bilby, hallo!"

Bilby saluted. Bilby was as precise as the antique watches he rebuilt at night in his basement. He was working on a vintage Longines when his neighbour's shed exploded in flames at 3 a.m. He phoned in the fire. Days later, Normal watched the professor cover the charred remains with plastic, tacking the corners with military precision. The shed's owner, an elderly widow, was sobbing.

"Nice day, Mr. Bilby," Normal squealed, his voice crackling like a bonfire. "I seen robins."

"Brilliant, Normal," replied Bilby.

"No, dey was robins."

❁   ❁   ❁

Arthur was waiting outside the recycle plant in soiled coveralls and work gloves.

"Can you bring da bus?" he asked. "We'll need it."

"Do monkeys play pianos?" Normal demanded.

"Straight up," Arthur shrugged.

Two university students walked by weighted down by backpacks. The girl's hair was pinned with asymmetrical clips, haphazard but composed, framing an angular face. Everything about her was as stark and vertical as a Modigliani painting. Arthur followed her with his eyes and then announced: "Wese going to have fun in Bumblefuck. Big got all the bling-bling."

Normal laughed, eyes squeezing shut behind the bulletproof glasses. He squealed until tears ran down his bristly cheeks.

❁   ❁   ❁

"If you go down in the woods today, you're sure for a big surprise." Normal was singing as Arthur pointed, through the darkness, to an unmarked road.

"This is it, fo' shizzle," he declared. "Da crib."

Normal turned the bus onto a gravel road, driving until he reached a chain strung between two posts. *Private Entry.* Arthur, who was wearing a faux-gold $$$ necklace and a baby-blue ball cap, hopped out and lifted the chain off its hooks. Normal killed the lights of the bus and drove blind as a sinner on the road to hell, the only sound the crunch of gravel.

He parked behind a cover of trees.

"I'm amped, hoes," snarled Arthur, who feigned a ghetto limp. "I'm amped."

Normal squinted, his eyes adjusting to the sight of a massive camp built on a river. It was owned by the town's richest man, dubbed, because of his three chins and vast wealth, Mr. Big. The camp glowed, a radioactive sprawl of redwood and illuminated windows, and it reminded Normal of a movie he had seen with blowsy blonds gathered around a piano at Christmas.

High as the angels in heaven, Arthur cursed, "There weren't supposed to be no one here."

"Well," Goose sighed. "Dere is."

A dozen cars surrounded the camp. Not knowing what to do, Normal tapped the hood of a Lincoln Town Car while Arthur contemplated the setback.

"I wouldn't buy no sissy car like dat," Normal vowed.

"What would you get?" asked Goose.

"I'd buy a camouflage Hummer wit' air," said Normal. "I'd jack her up so high—wit da central tire inflation system—dat I could drive rite over dat sissy car. *Boom*! Hummer Attack!"

"Won't dat bust your Hummer?"

"You can't bust a Hummer. Dat's why it's da toughest SUV in the world."

On their bellies, the three men crawled toward the camp and peered through a window. Inside, Mr. Big was surrounded by guests and waiters bearing trays of finger food. The tycoon's face dropped from his ears to his shoulders, with his three chins trapped in a freefall of fat. From their hiding spot, the would-be thieves could see the Champlain president and a host of woolly professors, befuddled by dactylic hexameter and iambic verse. All around the room were alumni with matching rings.

"How come dey're all here?" asked Normal.

"Big's a human rainbow, hoe, da pot of gold," Arthur said. "Big got all da bling-bling."

Before he struck it rich, Big had resided in the sticks near

Arthur. He had been married to a country girl named Tammi who had curling iron imprints in her hair. She was a romantic who placed a newspaper ad on their tenth anniversary. *Happy Birthday, my anniversary my darling Duff. Ten years, you planted the seeds in my heart, then watered them. It produced our beautiful daughters, Chrysalsis and Ericka. Forever yours.*

After Big made his fortune and became a university patron, Tammi was banished to a nearby town where you could openly enjoy the all-you-can-eat Chinese buffet and pose, without reprisal, for your engagement photo in a hot tub.

Normal glanced over his shoulder at Goose, who had managed to pry open a shed and was going through the contents. Through the camp window, Normal spotted Bilby and his finicky daughter, just back from an ashram in India. Last week, during the popcorn campaign, Normal knocked on Bilby's door as he always did. Bilby was good for a one-tin order. The daughter answered. She had to know him, Normal figured: Driver of the Month, top popcorn salesman, political pet, and yet she barely gave him room to speak through a crack in the door. Ignoring the snub, Normal informed her, "Your daddy always gets da Christmas tin." He paused to catch his breath. "Da one with da fat Santa on it. After you done wit da popcorn, you can use dat tin for smokes or marbles..."

The daughter glowered, and Normal feared that she would turn him down like the buzzard who lived next door, the old biddy who told him, "I can't eat popcorn. It gives me indigestion." Normal often cried, when his bus ran out of gas or when he spilled a box of tators like a broken strand of pearls, and when he left the biddy's house, his face was wet with tears, not tears of sorrow but the red-hot tears of rage.

"I don't want your popcorn," the daughter hissed, "and I know what you're up to. My father may not believe it, but I do."

Normal imagined himself behind the wheel of a Hummer, driving through Chatterville and flattening grand homes filled with oil paintings, Apple laptops, and ruling-class assumptions. People who gave him used clothes and patronizing smiles. He thought about how the storm in his head—swirling and bouncing—had calmed when he lit the old biddy's shed and the flames ignited. For a glorious moment, it was like being at a weenie roast with marshmallows on the end of a branch, and the static vanished like someone had attached a pair of rabbit ears to the sides of his skull.

"Dey ain't gonna leave," Normal told Arthur.

And then to Goose: "Go get dat gas can."

Normal had only planned on robbing Mr. Big, splitting the booty with Arthur, but the storm in his head was mounting. Normal wanted to own a Hummer and a camp and go to MMA fights and NASCAR races. He wanted to sell so much popcorn that someone would name a university building after him, just like Big. And then he felt the red-hot tears of rage.

Normal look a final look inside the camp. The room was decorated with photographs of Big receiving his honorary degree, Big doing a victory lap of the Champlain University rink with Zamboni Man, Big with alumni. Years of grooming had turned Big into a Madame Tussaud dummy of himself, with poreless skin and roseate cheeks.

Arthur, Normal noticed for the first time, had a bayonet in his hand. Goose had found a gas can in the shed.

"Let's light her up," Normal panted. "Let's light her up."

"Diggity dank!" said Arthur as the fire slowly started. "Diggity dank."

"If you go down in the woods today, you're sure for a big surprise," Normal sang, laughing so hard that tears ran down his bristly cheeks.

A Great Nation

Blake wore a hockey jacket and a pink Lacoste polo, collar popped. He hit all of the parties, where he preyed on drunken guests and had, it was widely known, molested a poor girl named Cortney, who was passed out in a car. No one tried to stop him.

Blake travelled in a pack with three smarmy friends in matching jackets. Freckled, with hair the colour of boiled squash, he audaciously strutted into school past the punks, the stoners, and the band geeks, who knew about the parties and, with a collective sense of injury, hated his guts.

Cortney lived in the same housing project as Paul. Paul was a petty criminal on Ritalin, a large boy with no impulse control who one day decided he didn't like the look of Blake. Paul wore a camouflage suit and a chin strap. A blunt behind his ear. On weekends, Paul fought rap battles and called himself the Sucka Free MC. "I'm beasted, I'm dope."

Paul sat on Blake's chest in the school parking lot near Mr. Piggott's souped-up Supra, and pounded him like he was throwing down insults. No one tried to stop him. The band geeks shuffled by in Ramones T-shirts; the gangstas shrugged; the smarms laughed nervously and pretended it had nothing to do with them.

Blake's father bought his son a pickup truck, a lawnmower, and a weed whacker to service neighbours' lawns. "He's running his own business," his father informed friends.

Blake drove the truck at high speeds though his suburb, frightening walkers and mothers with strollers. When cars passed, he invariably, in the manner of someone who thought too much of himself, turned to see if anyone had noticed him.

Paul battled a dude named Daynjr G, who was small and scared. It was three rounds, two minutes each, posted on YouTube.

"I'm six three," Paul fired his opening shot. "You're a pygmy."

The crowd howled as Paul tore down Daynjr G like a one-man demolition crew. He rhymed *feminine* and *gremlin*. Daynjr G flailed back with trash about Paul's momma, but it was as weak as his hand signals. Paul spent his two-hundred-dollar purse on Colt 45s and weed.

And then while Blake was picking his college residence and Paul was composing his next dope battle, a freak named Roach banged his face against a brick wall in Canadian history class. The class had already started when Roach, aged nineteen, arrived. They had finished Unit 7: *Canada: The Fifties & Sixties*. The door was locked, so Roach, who wore a spiked collar and a derby, kicked it with his jackboots. He licked the door's window.

Roach was short and ashen; the sides of his head were shaved. He lived alone. Some people thought he was a Satanist; others said he was "super religious" or maybe "mental." He worked weekends as a dishwasher at Swiss Chalet. Mr. Piggott let him in and someone shouted: "Hey Roach, why don't you bang your head against the wall?" Roach smashed his forehead on the brick. It made an odd-sounding crunch. Someone laughed.

And then, to show the randomness of life, the swirling currents of angst and isolation, Roach smashed his face over and over again until his nose cracked with a sound that should have been louder, and in reality was so muted that only a girl in the front row clearly heard it. No one tried to stop him, and when it was over, Mr. Piggott told the class to open their texts to Unit 8: *Canada: A Great Nation to Live In.*

Maury

Marta was watching Maury from her bedroom futon. The silver-haired TV host had four prototypical shows, she had decided: the paternity test show, the lie detector show, the can-you-tell-if-it's-a-he-or-she? show, and the out-of-control teenage girls.

Today it was the teens, jelly-bellied and belligerent, appearing on a screen under the title: *My Thirteen-Year-Old Daughter Is Trying to Get Pregnant!* When the teens hit the stage to a howl of condemnation, they gave the audience the finger: "Shut the fook up! You dohn know me you dohn know me." They spoke in an American dialect that reminded Marta of tenements and drive-by shootings, a part of America she had never seen but knew was powerful enough to change the way people talked.

There was one girl, Tashonda, whom viewers were meant to hate, and during her time on stage she kept a baby soother in her mouth. Not only was she attempting to get pregnant, the audience was informed, but she beat her little sister, whose picture was then displayed. "Shut the fook up. You dohn know me!"

Tashonda's mother sobbed with each revelation: Sex for money. Sex with thirty men. What, Marta wondered, was next?

"Is it true you stole fifty dollars from your grandmother's purse when you visited her in the hospital?" Maury asked.

"Yeah, I done that."

The mother collapsed to the floor.

The girls were all doughy and unattractive, ensuring that the studio audience—the same people titillated by the antics of Paris Hilton or Kim Kardashian—would despise them on sight. The girls had pulled-back hair and modest IQs, and they responded in four-beat outbursts of defiance.

Marta smiled when Preshess mooned the crowd. The audience—themselves poorly dressed—lunged from their seats, ready to stone Preshess as an agent of Satan, eager to shift the blame for their own failures to a stage full of wretched, disadvantaged, and vulgar teens, incapable of understanding the tragedy of their lives.

Marta felt her neck tingle before she heard her stepfather's unctuous voice.

"They're all actors, you know."

Marta kept her eyes on the TV.

Her stepfather was in the doorway along with Marta's mother, Penelope, and he looked pleased with himself, as though he had just solved the mystery of the grassy knoll. Marta ignored Kim and stared at the television, which showed LaRhonda sitting like an old man in suspenders, legs spread to accommodate a gut. LaRhonda had just admitted to having sex in her mother's bed with a forty-year-old man.

Penelope announced airily: "We are going to The Exhibit. Oliver *needs* to be walked."

Marta shrugged; it was the first time she had laid eyes on her parents in days, and she blinked, trying to familiarize herself with them. Kim—both adults insisted on being called by their first names—was wearing full Lululemon; Penelope was swathed in a bawdy shawl pinned by a silver brooch that was allegedly inspired by an eleventh century archaeological find in Scandinavia.

As the front door closed and Kim started up his Volvo, Marta reached under her bed for the bottle. She took two enormous swigs, and waited for the vodka to soothe her nerves, to take the edge off the loneliness. Her loneliness felt like a form of brainwashing, a slow torture that rendered her so disoriented that time had no meaning, her emotional clock set only by Maury, who appeared, like a loyal friend in a V-neck and slacks, each weekday at 4 p.m.

❀   ❀   ❀

The Exhibit—as Penelope grandly called it—was a display of art submitted by people who had received medical treatment for mental illness. It was organized by Kim's employer, a government department entrusted with culture and wellness. To encourage participation, the department had mounted posters in various locations, including the Salvation Army homeless shelter. The posters featured Van Gogh's *Self-Portrait With Bandaged Ear* from 1889. "Van Gogh was mentally ill!" the script proclaimed over the artist's face. "*We are inviting all mentally ill people to submit their artwork for a special contest.*"

Kim had collected the fourteen exhibit entries and posted snapshots of them on the department website. Curious, Marta visited the site. She especially liked the watercolour painted by the lady who had changed her name from Elaine to Elan, and she enjoyed the folk-art carving of a matador made by a man named Buck.

Kim—an artist with more refined sensibilities (according to himself)—had deliberated about whether to admit the papier mâché totem pole two days late. He had finally agreed to accept it, along with an acrylic painting of a moose standing in front of a cabin on a lake. The long-legged moose reminded Marta of the AT-AT walkers from *Star Wars*.

"I am making an exception," Kim had scolded the moose painter, a man named Virgil.

"Mmmmm," Virgil murmured.

"I am doing you a *favour*."

Virgil did not respond, so Kim informed him, "You will get your name tag the day of." Kim gestured toward a co-worker named Donna, who was making the name tags which were shaped like apples and contained the words: *EXHIBITOR, Mentally Ill.* Donna had a collection of frogs on her desk: ceramic, pewter, and clay; some were wearing dresses and top hats, others had their legs splayed like Cossack dancers. Virgil hobbled away, and then when almost out of earshot, muttered: "Ribbit."

Marta watched the remainder of *Maury* and shuffled to the end of her street. Marta lived in a working class area near a defunct sanatorium and a former orphanage. A few stone townhouses and postwar bungalows had been taken over by trendies who worked in the downtown core. They drove bicycles or small foreign cars; they wore fanny packs and Mountain Equipment Co-op shoes, hats with ear flaps, and South American mittens.

Marta boarded the bus. Across the aisle sat a man and his daughter, who was little more than a baby. The father's arm was draped protectively around the girl. On his shoulder was an elaborate tattoo of two men in ball caps staring into space, both giving the world the finger. The faces appeared copied from a photo booth picture and were captioned: *Brothers for Life.*

On an optimistic day, Marta imagined the father vowing "to get off the weed and earn my GED." She imagined him taking the little girl swimming. The girl turned to stare at Marta, and the father copied her, seeking approbation. He wore hoop earrings and a chrome chain that looked too heavy for his bony chest.

Other people's anxiety made Marta anxious; pitiful people made her overwhelmingly sad, and she saw—in vivid colour—the trips they would never take, the loved ones they had lost in highway crashes. She saw bare mattresses on apartment floors and blue liqueur bottles placed on window sills as decor. Marta studied the pair, knowing that sometimes, people are at *that* point in time where everything has stacked up against them and they are crumbling, decomposing, into a splotchy heap of nerves and angst and utter despair. At this nadir of their existence, they needed hope, they needed grace, they needed a touch of kindness, and it can all turn or collapse at that moment in time. Marta smiled at the girl, who, instead of smiling back, stared with the emotionless face of a martyr.

Marta entered the medical clinic and took a seat in the waiting room. She smiled at the room, and after getting little response, turned her thoughts to Preshess. After *Maury* had ended, Marta had tried on a tube top and cut-off shorts and paraded in front of a full-length mirror, shouting: "Shut the fook up! You dohn know me, you dohn know me!" practising the intricate neck swivel. Marta wished she could be as insolent as Preshess, who barricaded her emotions behind a wall of belligerence, protected from the rashes and stomach problems that Marta suffered.

The walls were bare except for one sign posted around the room: *Absolutely No Food or Drinks Allowed in Waiting Room.* It seemed unnecessarily cruel to the hacking wretches with scratchy throats and scorching temperatures heading into their third straight hour of sitting.

The receptionist's desk was enclosed in Plexiglass with a hole for patients to speak through; it reminded Marta of *Silence of the Lambs.* Outside the glass, a sloppy patient in earmuffs greeted every arrival with "You just go up there and get a number and then you wait like the rest of us..." People ignored the old woman, who babbled: "I have a hernia, ya know, and the diabetes."

"I could be dead, ya know, if I don't get in there."

"I was supposed to be babysitting four kids." A claim that raised eyebrows.

Disappointed with the room's failure to engage, she turned to a mother cradling a feverish toddler, and asked, as if to show her maternal instincts: "How is he?"

The mother shrugged.

"Is he alive?" she asked.

The mother nodded yes, and then reached into a satchel and pulled out a bottled water, which she pressed to the toddler's lips.

"No drinks allowed." The greeter pointed at the sign. "Not your fault, not your fault."

The receptionist called Marta's name.

Kim was in the habit of bringing every conversation back to one of two topics: himself, or the importance in society of "proper footwear." Kim had a low opinion of anyone who did not wear Birkenstocks or Mephistos. He and Penelope also took pride in their disdain for fried food, rightwingers, and whatever Republican devils were destroying the world. Reality TV was also diabolical, though Marta did not understand how it was connected to the other social crimes.

Before she had married Kim, Penelope had lived with a woman named Regina. Regina wrote a newspaper column that she used, regardless of the purported topic, to attack unwary members of her family living in Saskatchewan. If the issue was Sunday shopping, she would endorse it, adding that she had never enjoyed cozy Sunday dinners because her mother, now dying of bone cancer, was always drunk by supper. If the topic was euthanasia, Regina would argue that her father, frail after a lifetime of being a domineering bully, was a good candidate. Marta thought that Regina's column was depressing and predictable, because readers knew that, after four paragraphs of social commentary, all of it politically correct and enlightened, they would be subjected to another dreary attack on Regina's defenceless relatives, who by the end of the day appeared sympathetic. Penelope and Kim never talked about Regina. They did, however, support some of her causes, including the plight of Ethiopian coffee workers, anti-globalization, and world peace.

Marta boarded the bus for home and took a window seat. She caught her reflection in a storefront and frowned. She was a ginger kid, the punchline for an entire *South Park* episode that depicted redheads as disgusting, inherently evil, and without a soul. She had no idea how many relatives shared this affliction because Penelope refused to discuss Marta's real father or his family tree. They were never to be mentioned.

Marta was asleep when the door slammed. She had been dreaming that she was in the clinic waiting room and she—not the mother—was being scolded by the messy woman, who repeated over and over "Not your fault, not your fault." Marta's chest tightened until she could barely breathe. Now, Marta heard her mother's voice rising in waves of outrage. "Can you believe those people? Can you believe them?" Kim muttered something inaudible, and Penelope's sobbing reached a frenzy—"Why did you *make* me go, Kim? Why? Now I just feel sick…"—and was interrupted by a low response from Kim, who retreated to the deck. The smell of marijuana drifted into the house.

Marta attempted to go back to sleep, but her mother's anger bumped against her bedroom wall after the noise had subsided. As though the air were made of glass, Marta willed herself still. She had no way of knowing why the exhibit had so enraged Penelope; she had no way of knowing that after the fourteen exhibitors had been told that their work would be featured on a calendar, a dealer named Gregor had approached Kim.

"Where is the artist of the moose painting?" Gregor asked.

"He's here *somewhere*," said Kim, wondering who had invited Gregor. "And he's not an artist."

"I'll be the judge of that," snipped Gregor. "Where is he?"

Virgil was standing in a corner. He had shown scant interest in the event and was wearing his *EXHIBITOR, Mentally Ill* name tag upside down. Virgil panhandled outside a coffee shop. In winter, his beard collected ice crystals and he crouched in the shadow of the building as if to ward off blows. "How are you, Virgil?" regulars would ask as the wind shoved pedestrians down the sidewalk, scattering newspapers and idle thoughts. Mute inside his hooded jacket, Virgil would nod as they dropped quarters in his cup. Sometimes, a boy with a face tattoo and a dog crouched on the opposite corner.

"Someone wants to speak to you," said Kim.

"Someone wants to stick a pole up your ass," replied Virgil, who laughed.

Virgil nonetheless followed Kim across the room, where Gregor offered the artist two thousand dollars for the moose painting, an overture which Penelope watched in disbelief, feeling—she later told Kim—as though someone had "ripped my heart from my body."

"It's brilliant," Gregor pronounced. "Just brilliant."

Penelope was a fabric artist who supported herself by teaching art at a community college. For twenty-five years, she had shown in libraries and co-ops; she had written critiques; she had attended every benefit that she could, all the while assuring herself she was too esoteric for the masses. None of that mattered, she had convinced herself, until now, when she realized in a crushing epiphany that she was, in the eyes of people like Gregor, an irrelevant failure who glued pieces of gingham to a board and called it art.

Virgil's soul-destroying sale could not have come at a worse time. All winter, Penelope had buried herself in her studio. Weeks before the exhibit, she had released her most daring work, a one-woman show that included a death rattle of gratuitous obscenities aimed at startling viewers. On top of the now-familiar gingham, Penelope had printed:

GINGHAM
Dog

Bow wow wow
Manchester mills
Fucking instrument of
capitalist oppression

bleed

Penelope had also mounted—on madras—photos of diseased genitalia she had clipped from medical journals: a shock attack of desperation.

Kim wrote a press release for Penelope's exhibit and emailed it to the newspaper and Gregor's gallery. Penelope posted a Wikipedia entry on herself using the same impenetrable language she used to explain her work, to give it meaning in lieu of visceral force.

As part of her rebranding, Penelope had traded her granny glasses for purple and green frames; she had grown out her buzz cut and added blocks of red. Penelope had an overwhelming desire to be part of *It* and was shattered when she realized that her identity, an identity more important than Marta or Kim, an identity that elevated her above the hoi polloi, was built on a single crumbling premise: that she was an artist. And now this crap with Virgil.

Marta heard a bowl smash, the soundtrack to the rage that accompanied all of Penelope's disappointments, failures she attributed to Marta, who had—if you believed Penelope—stalled her ascent, stifled her creativity, and ruined her life until she had salvaged something by marrying the sexually ambivalent Kim.

Marta took another drink of vodka. She turned on her laptop and tapped the keyboard. "Not your fault, not your fault, not your fault..." Of late, the loneliness felt unbearable and all of her senses activated at once, bouncing against each other like nightclub patrons caught in a fire, panicking and trampling, the exit obscured. In the low light, Marta composed her salutation, having found the address on the Internet where you could locate anything these days.

Dear Maury:

Marta thought about the man on the bus and how he kept one tattooed arm around his daughter as though she was precious, as though he knew he was prone to careless missteps he could not afford to make. Marta wondered if the girl was named Angel or Heaven or Desiree, and then she heard music that sounded like an ice cream truck. Marta restarted her letter:

To the Producers of Maury:

I would like to appear as a guest on your show. At the age of fifteen, I believe I have found, after an exhaustive search, my long-lost father, whose name is Franki Binns. I went to a medical clinic and requested a DNA test. They told me they do not do them. Now, I am turning to Maury. I believe that I would make an excellent guest on your show because my father—a man with the same red hair as me— is incarcerated in a federal penitentiary in British Columbia and can be easily reached. In photos, we bear a striking resemblance. I can leave at any time. It is in the best interests of everyone that you do not contact my mother, who cannot be trusted, particularly in matters involving my paternity.

Your most loyal fan!!!

Marta Marche

Jess Loves Jorge

She had a look I couldn't define: too pale, too modestly attired, in opaque glasses and hair that had never been styled. The kind of person you would see arriving at a religious convention held in a sports arena, clad in her Sunday best, part of a cavalcade of subdued women and teens in frilly dresses. The women two steps behind the men, slowed by coolers and blankets. She looked like that, except there was something in her eyes you couldn't pin down, something people would try to describe when she later drowned her three children in a bathtub then sat waiting for her husband to come home.

And I was wrong about the woman: she had never been married.

Just after Christmas, she boarded a plane for Florida where she was met by a stocky man named Jorge, a forty-five-year-old Colombian who worked in a restaurant and had met her online. The kind of man who liked Alfa Romeos and *aguardiente*.

In Florida, she posted Facebook photos of herself blissfully drunk in a bar, and on a beach, sun-soaked. "I love my Jorge," she swore in the cutline. Squinting without glasses, a wet T-shirt over her bathing suit. Carefree. She looked like that, except there was still something in her eyes you couldn't pin down, something people would try to describe when they found her.

The woman's name—the newspaper reported—was Jessica Rutledge, and she was twenty-four years old. She had grown up in Myer's Cove, Nova Scotia, about a two hours' drive from Halifax. She loved country music and dogs. She had graduated from Myer's Cove Consolidated High School. She had a seven-year-old son named Laughlin.

"She was an angel from heaven," her mother told the newspaper. "She and Jorge were soulmates."

Jorge Gonzalez's official obituary made no mention of Jessica or seven-year-old Laughlin. It did say that Jorge had graduated from high school in Ibague, Colombia. He had reached a long-time goal by becoming an American citizen; he was an ardent student of Colombia's Vallenato music. He was Catholic.

"Jorge was an amazing cook who liked to entertain."

The story appeared in the news because of the freakish way in which the pair died: killed when a carnival ride named the Octopus malfunctioned at a county fair in Formosa, Florida. The couple fell ten metres when their car crashed to the ground. The paper ran a photograph of the Octopus—named after an eight-footed cephalopod with no internal skeleton—and the ride had six arms, all painted fluorescent green. It was was owned by Fantasy Midway, and it moved between fairs and exhibits. "This is the first accident of this kind with the Octopus," a Fantasy spokesperson told the media. "It is usually a very safe and popular ride."

Jorge and Jessica were taken to hospital, the paper reported, but died from internal injuries. Laughlin, who had been seated between the adults, miraculously survived.

On the day of the accident, the fair had been hosting a baby contest, and thirteen infants competed in the Teeny Tiny Miss Formosa Fair Category (0–6 months) with judging based on Appearance, Personality, and Presentation. Despite the tragedy, the contest was successfully completed, and the winner received a crown and a trophy.

Laughlin, who had spent most of his life in the company of his mother, was an odd boy with flashing eyes and a habit of interrupting conversations with random comments.

"Where are you going?" he had asked Jorge earlier that day.

"Nowhere."

"If you were really going nowhere, you would not be moving. You would be standing in one place. Heh heh heh."

"All right, Laughlin."

"If you were standing at the centre of the Earth, you would burn up because it is three thousand degrees Celsius."

"I will try not to go there."

People agreed that Laughlin was unusual. Some surmised his mother had encouraged Laughlin's unsolicited displays of knowledge, believing they were proof of a superior intelligence. Some said he had an abnormal aptitude with computers and could use one by the time he was five. He collected pop bottle lids and had, before he moved to Florida, 497 of them.

"All porcupines float when they are in water."

Sometimes, during his monologues, Laughlin would stop and tilt his head back, mouth agape. The pauses could last twenty seconds, and it seemed as though Laughlin were downloading files to his overworked brain, waiting for them to open.

"The Brown Hairy Dwarf Porcupine lives in Venezuela. Heh heh heh."

Jess and Jorge's deaths prompted an inquiry, which, like most inquiries, seemed based on the premise that there is no such thing as an accident or bad luck. The U.S. Consumer Product Safety Commission stated that over twenty-five hundred people a year are injured in rides that move across the country, and regulation of the movable rides varies greatly from state to state. An inspector determined that a bracket on the Octopus had snapped from excessive wear.

Someone flew Jess's mother to the inquiry, and she talked to reporters outside the building. The fatal day, she told them, had started off like any other. Jess and Jorge had taken Laughlin to a flea market, one of those places where you could purchase Confederate flags and Southern Pride stickers. They bought the boy a ten-dollar novelty bike helmet in the *Pickelhaube* design made famous by the Prussian Army. Laughlin owned a bicycle, which he drove down sidewalks at high speed, brushing strangers.

"He has so much energy," the grandmother sighed.

Jess had quit her job at Pete's Pizzeria in Florida before the accident, her mother said, and she and Jorge were thinking of starting a business.

"She said she was tired of working for other people," her mother explained. "She had all kinds of ideas. She was considering starting a personal shopping business or a dog grooming operation. She had *so* many ideas."

Jessica and Jorge loved the zoo. Jessica had learned how to make clam linguini.

Jessica's mother started a Facebook group entitled *In Memory of Jess and Jorge,* which she filled with pictures of the doomed couple in Florida. The Florida Jessica bore little resemblance to the hopeless woman I had seen in Nova Scotia. She was tanned with white sunglass circles around her eyes. Her hair was in a ponytail. She no longer looked like a woman whose heart had been broken so many times that all that remained was scar tissue.

In one picture, she was standing on a beach, and in the sand, she had written *Jess Loves Jorge*. In another picture, she was hugging Laughlin, who seemed unmoved by his mother's euphoric state, as though he had learned like most children to love his parent without question or cause. She was hugging him so hard that he looked in danger of collapsing.

Most of the Facebook posts were by Jessica's mother, who seemed determined to validate the couple.

"My darling daughter Jess, I am so relieved that you will be with Jorge forever. You were the perfect couple and will remain so for all time. Xxoo"

Two days later:

"Dear Jess. You are a Princess and Jorge is your Prince. I know that Jorge will look after you in Heaven where you are safe and happy. Laughlin sends his love."

There were two comments from the public:

"I went to high school with Jessica and she was always nice to me," wrote Melanie Baker from Myer's Cove.

"Love you sweet baby," wrote Heavenlii Jones, a waitress at Pete's Pizzeria. Heavenlii's motto was *Livin Da Good Life*.

No one seemed to care that Jessica's mother had not seen her daughter for two years, or that all Jessica had wanted, like legions of girls around us—plain girls, pretty girls, smart girls, and fools— was to be loved. That shouldn't, I decided, be so implausible; it shouldn't be so fantastic.

Fantasy Midway paid Jess's mother a settlement of eighty thousand dollars, and she brought Laughlin back to Nova Scotia to live in Myer's Cove. She put a computer in his room and bought him a bicycle, which he drove down sidewalks at high speed, brushing strangers. Laughlin was not allowed to wear the *Pickelhaube* helmet because it did not meet provincial regulations.

Laughlin was obsessed with a comic book character named the Lizard, a villain who appeared in the *Spiderman* movie and video games. The Lizard was originally an Army surgeon whose arm had been amputated. After studying the biology of reptiles able to regenerate limbs, the Lizard found a way to grow back his own arm, inadvertently turning himself, through a scientific miscalculation, into a reptile man with superhuman strength.

"The Lizard can lift twelve tons."

"The Lizard possesses a six-foot tail, which he can whip at speeds up to seventy miles per hour."

And then, in his only allusion to the freakish accident that had taken his mother's life—and reshaped his as profoundly as bad science had redefined the surgeon's—he announced: "An octopus can regenerate a lost arm, though octopi with missing arms are fairly common."

Laughlin tilted his head back, mouth agape, before continuing: "The blue-ringed octopus is one of the most dangerous known creatures and carries enough venom to kill twenty-six people within minutes."

At the inquiry, the public learned that Jorge had grown up in Ibagué, which calls itself the Musical City of Colombia. The surrounding countryside is fertile, producing coffee, tobacco, and sugarcane. When Jorge moved to Florida, he brought a guitar and a coffee press. He had dreams of a music career. Jess, they learned, loved karaoke.

About a year before she met Jorge online, Jess had moved from Myer's Cove to the frayed hem of Halifax. She got a counter job at Harvey's. Laughlin attended an elementary school and, during lunch, sat in a corner by himself with his eyes closed, pretending to play a plastic recorder.

It was a neighbourhood of vinyl-sided houses and high rises occupied by single mothers and call-centre workers. There were a disproportionate number of limps and breathing problems. Jess and Laughlin lived on the second floor of a three-storey walk-up. On one side was a Sally Ann Resource Centre, on the other a Kentucky Fried Chicken that advertised "Simpson Figure with Family Meal" and was the scene of a scuffle when it ran out of Barts.

None of the apartments had real curtains—just sheets, pink, blue, or floral—and none of the occupants operated on a regular schedule. A man who lived below Jess opened the front door three or four times a night and stared down the street. Usually, he was wrapped in a blanket, one of those cheap ones that the airlines hand out for completing a survey, and on his feet were duck slippers. One night, while he was staring down the street, someone shot him. Laughlin saw a police car under his window and said: "The average person swallows eight spiders per year while sleeping."

Last night, I saw a scrawny girl inside a NEEDS convenience store one block from where Jess and Laughlin lived. She was wearing a low-cut top and she was holding hands with an American sailor who reminded me of baseball games and parades. She wore earrings that could, if you believed in fairy tales, have been from Tiffany.

I thought about Jessica posing outside a stucco house in Florida holding a sign: *I am living the dream.* It was the same dream that sent poor girls downtown when the fleet arrived. There was the chance that someone new, someone foreign, would see the special part of you that local boys missed, and he would whisk you off to a perfect place with sunshine and sandy beaches, where you could raise babies and go dancing on Saturday night. Did it ever really happen?

Unlike the lanky blond boys in white sailor suits—boys named Chip and Jackson—Jorge had a greasy face and pocked skin. He had three children who lived with a woman named Maria. The stucco house was in a public housing project that offered a course in lifestyle skills to children and adults after 4 p.m. It had a zero-tolerance policy.

The sailor bought the girl a Diet Pepsi, and she looked so happy that I thought she might cry. She looked like a girl who wore her heart on her sleeve.

Freud's Rat Man Was Conflicted

My father grew rich on the backs of rats and roaches and silverfish. They built him a big house with a fifty-foot pool and a three-car garage. On a sultry night when the air is close and judgmental, he hovers like a malignant demon, all ego and ire.

The next day, he crashes to Earth when the garbageman leaves him a form letter noting the improper disposal of pesticide cans. "Does he know who he is talking to?" demands my father, who cruises outside the garbageman's home in his unmarked truck, brutish and bent on revenge. "Does he fucking know?"

My sister tells everyone that she hates him. That's why she slashes her arms with razors and knives and other devices better directed at him.

He tells my sister that she's too fat for gymnastics.

He calls her a pig.

My sister shows her teammates her lacerated arms; she says she got fourteen stitches last year and spent three weeks in hospital. Inside, they talked about eye movement desensitization and stress. She's on meds now, she confides, her face so dark and glowering that it scares the other girls.

With everything tilting in one direction, the girls lurch to safe themes. They tell my sister that sometimes they drink coolers and they show her where they stash them. She tells the coach, and now they're suspended. "I'm rich as fuck," she boasts, sounding just like him.

Besides his pest control empire, my father owns a nursing home and a par-three golf course. He tells his clients that my sister is going to the Olympics. He's president of her club and the whole provincial association. No one will run against him.

A shrewd businessman, he keeps an office in our house which allows him to deduct lights, heat, and household expenses. To satisfy the tax people, he stores an electric fogger, double-ended traps, and poisons in a shed by the pool.

My sister tells a new girl—a vaulter named Rina—that our mom's an alcoholic. She tells Rina that she slashes her arms with razors and knives and other devices better directed at him, and then she hammers Rina from behind, fracturing her arm.

I did the math.

Rats have litters of six to twelve and young rats can reach reproductive maturity in three months. Breeding is most active in spring and fall. The average female has four to six litters per year. Rats can live eighteen months, but most die before one year. There are no rats in here, just nurses and doctors who try to force food down my throat, not seeing that I am growing fatter each day until I will become as huge and greedy as my father.

Before I got too fat for gymnastics, he would sit at my gym and watch me train. I felt like a bug he could crush at any time. Grinning like a good old boy, exchanging niceties with unwary parents, making small talk about fishing and the weather, pretending that nothing mattered when nothing mattered more. Sometimes, he wore oversized jeans and suspenders to appear disarming. The most successful exterminators are discreet and cold-blooded.

Freud's Rat Man was obsessed with rats and a grisly form of torture, a condition recorded in the case study published in German. *Bemerkungen über einen Fall von Zwangsneurose* (Notes Upon a Case of Obsessional Neurosis). Rat Man, the public name that the patient was given by Freud, was conflicted about his father. Had he wanted him to die or not?

Rat Man's father was probably more deserving of life than mine.

Only the rats can stop my father, it seems. Human devices like reason and moral boundaries will not work. Like the rats, he has no conscience. If you cross him, he will pay a hacker to invade your online life; he will poison your cat, stalk your children over minor disagreements that others would shrug off. Pretending to be lost, he will stroll into your workplace with his bug-killing crew. Norway rats are husky, brownish rodents that weigh about eleven ounces. They are about thirteen to eighteen inches long including the six- to eight-inch tail.

A rat's incisor teeth grow one-half inch per month. These teeth are harder than steel and are attached to jaws that exert a pressure of seven thousand pounds per square inch. They can gnaw through sewer pipes or walls. Rats will eagerly feed on humans if they are still or unconscious; rats eat babies in their cribs.

My mother drinks until she drops like a fumigated roach. Sometimes my father leaves her on the floor; sometimes he tells my sister to pick her up. When he watches my sister train, he smiles his good old boy smile while his eyes track her like a red-beamed laser. My sister is stronger than I am. My doctor says I have gymnast's wrist, which causes a premature closure of the growth plates. According to my specialist: "Repeated stresses affect the distal radial growth plate, causing undergrowth of the radius, and a resultant ulnar-plus variance." The normal treatment is wrist splints, but severe cases require arthroscopic debridement. I may have a permanent deformity.

When my sister lost provincials to a girl named Nelle, my father bought her a VW bug convertible as a statement. Pink, with a vanity plate that said: GYMRAT. My sister drove to Nelle's school and offered her boyfriend a ride. They had sex, she told everyone, in a parking lot near the river. She let him drive.

Freud's Rat Man, now believed to be a young lawyer named Ernst Lanzer, was killed in World War One, precluding any follow-up on his case. Although Freud wrote extensively about his patient—disagnosing melancholia, obsessional neurosis, and a father complex—I wonder: did Rat Man have more to say?

Last night, they made me eat. When they force food on me, I feel a panic in my chest as though I am trapped in a cell, imprisoned by flesh. Sometimes the panic, which revs and races like a caffeine attack, lasts for hours, sometimes for days. Rats can hide in piles of firewood, overgrown shrubs, old mattresses, or discarded furniture. They are cunning.

I will not let them feed me again. I am tough enough to win. While I was competing, I had a herniated disc and a hyper-extended knee. I don't believe the scales, which say I weigh eighty-seven pounds. When the doctors show me the numbers, I nod, refusing to be tricked. I can feel the fat on my body, oppressive and suffocating like a snowmobile suit, zipped tight with an eight-ounce liner. It chokes me.

In the Chinese city of Tangshan, someone sprinkled rat poison on breakfast food served at the Heshengyuan Soy Milk snack shop, killing forty people and sickening three hundred more. Police arrested the owner of a rival restaurant. In parts of China, murder by rat poison is so rampant that the government is raiding homes and arresting citizens who harbour the poison.

Rodents are difficult to kill with poison because they are scavengers. They eat a tiny amount and then wait. If they don't become ill, they continue. An efficient rodenticide must be tasteless and odourless in lethal concentrations, and have a deferred effect.

Our shed is full of rodenticide and little by little, my sister is putting it in his food, titrated to the right dose and time period. It's a slow killer. A superwarfarin that thins the blood and causes internal hemorrhaging.

Sometimes the brain bleeds slowly and imperceptibly, like a bird caught in a trap.

Johnnycanuck
Had This
to Say

Not everything is how it appears. Not every villain you see on the TV news is a menace to society, a human wrecking ball, a social misfit bent on wreaking havoc. Some, like myself, James Arthur Bungay, are ordinary people who have, through no fault of their own, been caught in a typhoon of duplicity and deceit, hurled—against their will—into an impossible circumstance. But now I am rambling. Yes, I did something stupid, something impulsive and out of character for a man like myself, and now they have me in their sights, and I must prepare to accept the consequences of my actions, if or when they find me.

But first, before you are exposed to a mélange of half-truths and lies of omission, here is my side of the story, my version of what drove me to such a desperate act.

I married young.

My mistake.

I married a woman I believed was "cool."

My mistake again.

I ignored the fact that she was eight years older than I was and, judging by the appearance of her mother, inclined to age as badly as a truffle soufflé.

Yes, I ignored that.

We were doing a fair bit of cocaine at the time and one night, after she caught me in bed with my best friend's ex—a lovely little makeup artist—I panicked, and said, "Let's just get married." I married the old battle-axe, and within five years people mistook her for my mother. What's worse, the wretched old beast had tricked me: she was *not* "cool;" her idea of a fun time was driving to Grandma's house on Grand Manan for a rollicking game of euchre.

Barbara. My wife's name is Barbara. It makes me sick just to say it.

Does that make me sound like a bad person?

I don't care, with the mess that I am in.

I just don't care.

Barbara was working as a stockbroker when we met. She was savvy and ruthless enough to earn six figures a year and drive a turbocharged Lotus Esprit with leather seats and a tinted glass roof. She *may*—and I have no actual evidence of this—have been pushing shares in a dubious gold mine in Indonesia, but she did fly us both to Prague to see the Stones.

Barbara—does the name alone not sound like a longshoreman clearing his phlegmy throat?—elected to stay at home after the birth of our only child, Priscilla.

It was fine for a while, because Barbara's compulsive mothering and re-bonding with her own primordial mother gave me ample time to continue visiting my favourite haunts. I love that word—*haunts*—a euphemism for dark bars and pickup joints, but I digress. If I am honest, and I am endeavouring to be nothing less than frank, the preschool years were fine. Just fine.

For a while, Barbara even had a friend. Our next-door neighbours were a young couple; he was a firefighter, she a stay-at-home mom. They had bought an old wooden house and added a swing and a dog. The couple went for long walks—in the rain, wind, and snow—with their dog and the baby carriage. They visited the library and the duck pond, and they came home each night to soup. They touched the walls of their home, feeling each bump and crevice, the fibre of their lives, remembering what it had been like to be latchkey kids, daycare survivors, caught in a frantic cycle of ambition. And then, to Barbara's disappointment, they got divorced and moved.

Life became problematic around the time that Priscilla entered Grade Two. Barbara had too much time on her hands. What was she supposed to do with herself and Priscilla? How could she fill all those hours? Why, music, of course, as though that was the only sensible answer. Music and amateur theatre would become their joint obsession.

Before I knew it, Barbara had become consumed—and that is not too strong a word—with children's choirs and acting, throwing herself and Priscilla into voice lessons and ghastly productions of *Hansel and Gretel*, studying piano so that she might, at some point, be able to accompany Priscilla.

I am going to stop for a moment and have a small drink of wine. Or maybe a large one.

I am back, feeling better. I don't know if I mentioned that I live in Moncton, which is, in my opinion, a deceptively chic city, a place where the women enjoy the *dernier cri*, and slip back and forth between two languages as effortlessly as they slip in and out of knee-high leather boots; a city where people like books and painters; a city which—despite the proximity of Magic Mountain—manages to be soigné.

Priscilla's voice was acceptable at best; she had also inherited the worst of both our families' looks. She got her red hair from my side of the family (it skipped me), and she got her squat frame—some might compare it to that of a medieval serf—from Barbara's side. Priscilla did not make a good first impression. She was a girl with oversized nostrils and teeth that did not fit; a girl who could never, no matter how much you loved her, and *I did love her*, be described as pretty. A girl who, under Barbara's direction, wanted to be on stage, which saddened me, knowing, as a man like me would, how cruel the world can be.

At the same time that Barbara and Priscilla were embarking on their doomed journey, my elderly mother was becoming more demanding. We lived about three kilometres apart, but my mother—a vortex of negativity and complaints—had a telephone which she used mercilessly, dialing up to ten times a day, disturbing what little peace I had managed to secure.

She would phone to tell me it was raining,

She would phone to tell me that her arthritic toe was acting up.

She would phone to tell me that Great-Uncle George had a gallbladder attack.

She would phone me to tell me that Gary Dalrymple, who had attended high school with me, had just been named to a utilities board in Ottawa.

"Good for Gary," I replied.

"It says in the newspaper that he graduated from UNB."

"Yes, that is true."

"It says that he worked with the Conservative party for four years in an important position."

"Great."

And then, in a pique of frustration: "You never got that contract, did you?'

Barbara decided to write a blog about Priscilla's nascent career, posting video clips of our daughter singing, following, I suppose, the lead of Justin Bieber's mother, who at least had a talent to work with. From time to time I forced myself to read the blog and the comments posted by Barbara's family.

"What a gift she has."

"She is a delight, an absolute delight."

"Please tell me when I can see her perform. She is so inspiring."

Barbara was turning Priscilla into the mirror image of herself, an arrogant and insufferable snob who believed she was better than her peers.

Did I mention that Barbara was short and squat? Or that sometimes when I saw Barbara scampering across a stage to give Priscilla directions, my mind played a horrible trick on me. I saw instead of my wife of twenty-two years, an orangutan, fist-walking, so low to the ground and fixated on a cluster of ripe mangoes that I blinked?

"Priscilla," I told a friend who mentioned the blog "is amazing." And then in a thin attempt at self-deprecation, "I don't know where she got it from."

Priscilla, who was named after Barbara's mother, was a gifted student, and I wish that Barbara could have left it at that, but in today's world it is not enough to be a good athlete or a good student or a good friend, because the media will remind you that someone—some composite of perfection, a superhuman amalgam—is not only an Olympic skier, but a PhD in rocket science. If you believe the news, we are surrounded by super-achievers, and if I were a kid today, I would retreat to my room with a videogame that would, at some point, tell me I was a winner. That's what I would do, but who am I to give advice, given the mess I am in today?

Barbara was too busy with amateur theatre to tend to any of the banal duties of our household, so she left them to me. She had me by the balls, because she knew that I had had an affair—okay, several affairs. She was exacting her revenge. I spent my days strapped to a BlackBerry, doing tasks not invented when I was a child. When I was a child, we had a milkman and a mailman. A pump attendant filled our car with gas and a teller cashed my father's cheque each Thursday. Doctor Webster came to our house when we had tonsillitis and Martin's Drug Store delivered our prescriptions in a green VW bug. Now I am running at one million miles an hour, doing the work of countless displaced people—ghosts—the beneficiary, I am told, of technology. It is no wonder that I drink six beer and half a bottle of Shiraz each evening just to cope. As an act of defiance, I refused to sort my recyclables last week, dumping twelve perfectly good wine bottles in the trash. *Je m'en fous.*

Last week, I tried to blow up a Toronto newspaper.

Or that's what they claimed.

I didn't really.

I simply had enough of this shit.

I will tell you what actually transpired, and it, like everything else, bears scant resemblance to the events depicted by the paper.

My mother lives next door to a politically active blind woman who is in the habit of staging protests outside bus terminals or office buildings, claiming that she has been discriminated against or denied access. She is also a bona fide nut, who disappears for extended periods of time, and during one of those disappearances, she left her dog tied outside.

My mother, being an incurable busybody, brought the dog in. I would have left the creature outside until its ears froze; I would have let the little bastard die, but my mother felt compelled to save it. She fed the dog and then waited for the neighbour to return, not saying a word to anyone.

And then, last Friday, my mother opened her newspaper and saw a front-page story: *Blind Woman's Dog Stolen.*

My mother phoned, demanding that I set things right.

"Jimmy, I didn't steal that dog."

"Okay."

"Tell them I have lived on this street for sixty years without having an ounce of trouble with anyone. Tell them that. Tell them that I have a pacemaker that is operating ninety-eight per cent of the time. I am pacemaker *dependent.*"

"They won't care, Mother. They won't care."

"How do you know if you don't try? How do you know *everything*?"

I found a phone number for the neighbour and left a message on her answering machine. She did not respond. I knocked on her door, but there was no answer. I called the police and they said they had no report of a stolen dog so they were not interested in talking to me. I called the newspaper, but the reporter, I was told, was on vacation.

The story got picked up, as they say in the news business. It made the *Globe and Mail,* The Canadian Press, and the CBC. Before we knew it, someone had started a Facebook group: Help Find Rusty, and someone had made a YouTube video, which included, to my surprise, a clip of the blind woman enjoying her celebrity while hiding from me and my mother.

And then—and this is where my life came undone, where I paid for every shortcut and moral transgression I have ever made— Edwin Barton stepped into the picture. Edwin Barton, pompous, smarmy dick, national columnist, bon vivant. From his pulpit twelve hundred kilometres away, Edwin pronounced that the "dog snatching" was symbolic of a declining sense of community in the far-flung parts of our country, backwaters devoid of community gardens and bike-share programs. He said the blind woman's dog was probably sold to a medical laboratory. "Could there be a more loathsome act, one that speaks more directly to the decline of social conscience?" he rhetorically asked.

I am pausing again to compose myself and calm my nerves with a drink.

I did not try to blow up Edwin's paper; I sent them an email saying they *should* be blown up, only because they refused to listen to reason, they refused to be fair, they refused—no matter how many times I asked them—to make things right.

Edwin's column attracted 426 online comments from the public. In case you have not noticed, there is an entire substratum of imbeciles out there, who spend twenty-four hours a day lashed to their computers, ready to write bombastic and uninformed comments under every story that appears online. Most are demanding vengeance, and some are cranks who bring every single topic back to their political agenda. A stolen dog and a blind woman? This was a gift from heaven.

Galileo44 had this to say: "No punishment is too excesive for this horible person. This is why Stephen Harper is getting tough with law and order."

The lynch mob railed on.

Dr. No: "Why is this not considered a hate crime? Blind people are a minority in our society. When this creep is brought to justice, this should be prosecuted as a hate crime."

Girliecue: "Only in No Funswick."

Johnnycanuck: "I lives in Moncton and I knows these people. There is more than meets the eye. I would not put nothing past the whole bunch of them, especially Jimmy. My sister lost two orange cats and this could be the reason for them disappearing. I hope the cops get their act together before more innocent animals is sold to them labs. They should leave people like me alone and go after this scum."

I attempted to post an online comment along with all of the others, but my comment did not get past the newspaper's moderator. I tried again. I then emailed Edwin, who fired back a flippant response. "Your intemperate tone speaks volumes." And then he tweeted: *The Dog Thieves Are Biting Back.*

I had several beers before I phoned Edwin's paper and asked to speak to an editor.

"Your story was wrong," I said. "I want a retraction."

"It's not a news story; it's a column."

"What difference does that make?"

"We stand behind our columnist, who is highly respected."

"Your columnist is an asshole."

"Sir, if you continue to use inappropriate language, I will be forced to terminate this call."

"We tried to give the dog back," I shouted. "We didn't sell it to a lab! And your columnist called my eighty-two-year-old mother loathsome. Isn't that inappropriate language?"

"It is not profane."

"Why do you let those idiots post comments that are not true?"

"Sir, we are providing a forum for public feedback."

"I'll fucking feedback you."

Click.

I am going stop for a moment and have another small drink of wine. Or maybe a large one.

Edwin's paper, you should know, is in the habit of mocking minor people or towns, targets that are doing nothing to bother them: raising chickens, holding snowmobile rallies, and surviving, inside broomball gyms and curling rinks, soul-crushing winters that could kill you. It's a cheap, transparent game. Last month, they wrote a feature on a Manitoba family with a rare genetic disorder and selectively included all of the details that made the family seem stupid and worthy of contempt. The reporter mentioned empty beer cans, rooms divided by bedsheets, and a mutt gnawing on a massive bone, the inference being that the family might have been spared if only they had been more cultured, more erudite, more like them.

After my run-in with the paper, Barbara assailed me. "Do you know how this could affect Priscilla's career?" she demanded. Do you know the sound that a car makes when the fanbelt is loose, that sharp squealing noise that lasts for ninety seconds after you leave your driveway? That was Barbara's voice.

"What career?"

"Her career as an artist. This paper has a major arts section and now you and your mother have offended the paper so that they will never write about Priscilla."

"The paper was not going to do a story on Priscilla. Are you crazy?"

"Not now, they won't. That's for sure."

I am not a criminal, a hothead, or a terrorist. I am fifty-year-old photographer, who once had artistic aspirations, but now makes a living shooting school portraits. I am not—in any sense of the word—volatile. I already admitted that I used to do cocaine in the eighties, but who didn't? And yes, I do have one friend who has a permit for medicinal marijuana—that *is* the law, you know—and flies to Amsterdam each year for a gathering of potheads who vote on the year's best strains, and yes, he returns with seeds in his luggage, but I am not Interpol, and what he does with his meagre cash crop is *his* business, not mine.

Did I tell you that last week, I got eyeglasses, and saw—for the first time—my true self in the mirror? It was staggering, really, because I had no idea that I had broken blood vessels on my nose, and that my hair, which I believed to be auburn, was almost grey.

Why did I get involved in this mess? Was it because my mother had harangued me, or was it the fact that no matter how annoying your mother may be, no matter what type of psychological warfare she uses upon you, you will, if you are any kind of man at all, defend her?

I am pausing for a small drink.

Did I tell you that I found Edwin Barton's photo and biography on the Internet?

The first thing I noticed about Edwin Barton were his lips: too large, too soft, too flaccid. I could never imagine those lips under a football helmet or a baseball cap. In command of a submarine or a fighter jet. They are the lips of the tall, aloof dickhead who stood in the back row of the school photo, believing he was better than everyone else, his eyes surrounded by bluish-black runoff.

In every current photo, Edwin is slouched in a chair, giving the impression that he is permitted to slouch because he is so special.

Edwin, I imagine, lopes about as though he were in *Brideshead Revisited*. He is thirty-three, married, with young two children named Molly and Noah. His wife is plain—I think she bears a striking resemblance to Virginia Woolf—but men like that do not care. I was that age once, when you are smug and foolish enough to believe that you have everything under control. Your children are too young to rebel, your parents too young to become a burden. You have, for the first time in your life, a house and a well-paying job, and you still believe that it is cute to stick your child's art in the front window of your house. Everything is going smoothly for a while.

I read as many of his columns as I could stomach.

Edwin believes that he is hip and plugged in, not realizing that his idea of hip is one generation removed from what is *in*. Nobody under thirty cares, Edwin, about compost heaps or Snuglis or bicycle lanes or farmers' markets and honey. Nobody cares. Nobody cares about pottery barns and strollers. Young people want to get drunk and get laid, Edwin. Even *I* know that.

And then Edwin's paper raised the ante by writing an editorial about animal cruelty, and I, like the stressed and irrational man I had become, fell for it. I got on a plane—I had been drinking heavily—and I flew to Toronto with a can of bear mace in my suitcase. Did I tell you that I was, in my younger days, a good-looking man? I am not being boastful; no one gets skunked at birth, we all get something to work with. I got looks and what did I do with them? When I was twenty, I had long brown hair, a thirty-one-inch waist, and people thought I looked like Jackson Browne, only taller. I had a high-school sweetheart named Marie-Pier and we went camping and we swam under a waterfall and built a fire and played guitar until the sky was as dark and blue as a new pair of jeans. I had a Leica M3 and she was beautiful, yes, beautiful...

Merde. I just heard a knock on my door and now I must be quiet. If I tell you anything else, I may endanger myself; I may inadvertently incriminate myself in a manner that could only be characterized as foolish. *Bonne nuit et au revoir pour maintenant, mon ami...*

ABOUT THE AUTHOR

Elaine McCluskey is the author of a short story
collection, *The Watermelon Social*, and a boxing novel,
Going Fast. A Journey Prize finalist, her award-winning
stories have appeared in many of Canada's leading literary
journals. A former bureau chief for The Canadian Press, she
worked as a journalist before turning to fiction. She teaches
journalism part-time and works as a writing coach.
She lives in Dartmouth, Nova Scotia.